A Thief in the Night

A Thief in the Night

By
JIM GRANT

MOODY PRESS
CHICAGO

For Myrna

Charlotte's Web, next to
the last sentence.

Keep a sharp lookout! For you
do not know when I will come,
at evening, at midnight, early
dawn or late daybreak. Don't
let *Me* find you sleeping.

JESUS CHRIST
Mark 13:35-36
The Living Bible

ONE

"And reports keep coming in from all over the globe confirming it as true. To say that the world is in a state of shock this morning would be to understate the situation."

At first it was just the fuzzy drone of the announcer that called Patty to consciousness. Her clock radio had switched on at ten, and the news sounded the same as always to her in her early stages of consciousness that morning.

But as her waking mind came into focus, so did the words the announcer was saying. Patty sat upright in bed, trying to brush away the last fingers of sleep.

"The event seems to have taken place at the same time all over the world—just about twenty-five minutes ago. Suddenly, and without warning, literally thousands, perhaps millions, of people just disappeared."

Patty was awake now, and her mind raced. A quick look toward the open bedroom door brought the sound of an electric razor to her ears.

"A few eyewitness accounts of these disappearances have not been clear, but one thing is certainly sure. Millions who were living on this planet last night are not here this morning!"

"Jim?" Patty called, almost hesitantly. Then, as though summoned by the sound of the razor, she crawled across the bed in a straight line to the open door.

"Jim?" she called louder, almost afraid of the answer she would hear. Still the razor and the announcer droned on.

"Speculation is running high that some alien force from outside our system has declared war on our planet. Some feel it to be a spectacular judgment of God."

8

Patty made her way cautiously down the hall toward the bathroom. "Jim?" she called again. It was the frightened, quiet call of one who already seemed to know there would be no answer. Perhaps the razor drowned out her call, but she called no louder.

Now she was at the bathroom door. She stopped before looking in. It was as though she had gone through the moment before, and this time did not want to find what she was about to find.

"The United Nations is in a special emergency session, as are the governments of most of the countries of the world. Reports coming in say that there are some members of nearly every government missing."

And now she looked in. And her face showed that it was as she had expected. In only a moment, her expression grew from total dispair to near hysteria. "Oh, no! No! Please, no! Please! No-o-o-o-!"

"Bishop Franklin Sullivan, Chairman of the Church Confederation, has proposed that this might closely resemble the rapture, spoken of in some areas of theology. He says, and I quote, 'Of course, even if it is something like the rapture, we need not panic. The very fact that we are here and able to discuss it, is sign enough that it is not all-inclusive.' End of quote."

The electric razor was plugged into the light fixture above the sink, and it swung in a slow pendulum motion over the taps. Its easy back-and-forth movement and constant tone seemed to mock Patty as she stared into the empty bathroom.

She turned, without shutting off the razor, and stumbled almost mechanically back toward the bedroom. As she approached the bed, the shadows in the folds of the pushed-in pillow where Jim's head had rested the night before almost appeared to be his head!

She rubbed her eyes and found them full of tears. A dullness was setting in; and her young, slender body seemed to sag with old age. It was as though she had cried for many hours, and now the tears came without the sense of sadness or pain.

She slumped down beside the bed and listened to the radio. Her mouth moved slightly as though she were reading the announcer's copy with him.

"The event spoken of in the Hebrew-Christian Scriptures is described somewhat in the gospel of St. Matthew, chapter twenty-four, verses thirty-six and on. Jesus Christ is reported to be the speaker and says, and I quote, 'But of that day and hour knoweth no man, no, not the angels of heaven, but my Father only.'"

And as the announcer continued reading the passage, Patty's mind traveled back to the first time she had heard those words. It had been at the state fair. She and her friends, Diane and Jenny, had looked into a tent which had been set up to resemble a coffee house. The music coming from a small group on the makeshift stage had been reasonably good, and the girls sat down to listen.

"This place is a trap," Diane whispered before

they had been there long. "This is some kind of-*religious* thing. Come on. Let's split."

Patty did not mind the religious overtones, but she would have left with her friends. It was Jenny, however, who kept them there. Either she did not realize they wanted to leave, or she pretended not to. The words of the song, and now those spoken by the lead singer, held her attention. Patty listened more closely to hear what was holding Jenny's attention.

"The world will be at ease," the young singer was reading from a paperback book in his hand. "Banquets and parties and weddings—just as it was in Noah's time before the sudden coming of the flood. People wouldn't believe what was going to happen until the flood actually arrived and took them all away. So shall My coming be."

Patty knew the story of Noah. "How long can you tread water?" echoed through her mind, and she smiled. But she had never thought of life just going on as usual back then. Somehow, what everyone *else* was doing while Noah was building the boat had never occurred to her. And besides, what was wrong with banquets and weddings?

"Two men will be working together in the fields, and one will be taken, the other left," the singer continued reading. "Two women will be going about their household tasks; one will be taken, the other left."

Diane stifled a giggle, catching Patty's attention. It was obvious that Diane had not been listening. She had made eye contact with a boy across the room

11

and had managed to cause him to pour his cola down the front of his shirt. Diane seemed to enjoy getting people to make fools of themselves—especially boys.

"So be prepared, for you don't know what day your Lord is coming."* The singer finished reading and lowered his book. He was obviously a better singer than reader or preacher, but his earnestness had a kind of charm to it that Patty liked.

"What does all this mean?" he asked quietly. "It means exactly what it says. Any minute. Any second could be the last chance anyone has to give himself to Jesus. When it happens, it will happen that fast." He snapped his fingers.

Diane giggled again, dividing Patty's attention. There were times when it was fun to watch Diane in action. She could fix a boy with a look that would not only turn him on but inside-out at the same time. But the boys who knew her had a name for her which Patty did not understand. She only knew it was not very complimentary. Diane rarely dated anyone more than once and had left a string of unhappy young men in her wake.

The boy with the cola-soaked shirt was in real trouble. His spill had attracted the attention of a girl at his table who was obviously more than a mere acquaintance. And beside the wet spot was a name badge identifying him as one of the people who was there to help those who might be seeking the experience the group was offering.

When Diane played her game, she was merciless.

* The Living New Testament

12

Seeing the boy's badge only spurred her on. She formed the words, "Will you save *me*?" with her mouth and sent them to the already shaken boy. He looked away, looked at his puzzled girlfriend, looked at the floor. And when his girlfriend looked in the direction of Diane and her friends, they were all looking at the singer; and no one was more transfixed in her gaze than Diane!

"The Bible says, 'in the twinkling of an eye.' Millions of people, true Jesus people, will disappear, leave this earth to meet their Lord; and a shocked world will discover suddenly that what the Bible said was true! This is no joke. This is not a fairy tale. It *will* happen, just as sure as you and I are here right now."

It must have been "this is no joke" that penetrated Diane's consciousness, because she threw a small negative reaction in the direction of the young singer. And when he said that the event would happen as sure as they were all there, Diane simply got up and left. Patty and Jenny followed.

The singer's last words also followed. "So Christian, be alert! And friend, if you haven't yet given your life to Jesus Christ, do it! Do it *now*, because the rapture *will* come, and Christ *will* return. It says so in the Bible. He will come as a thief in the night—"

The sun flashed into Patty's eyes as the three walked out onto the midway. Its brightness seemed an odd punctuation to the singer's words. But soon her eyes were adjusted, and her ears were filled

13

with the sounds of calliope, children, screams and laughter; and the singer seemed so far away in that dark tent as to be no more important than any other attraction at the fair.

For some reason, Patty was unusually aware of faces, They appeared to be almost an illusion; laughing children's faces, screaming people's faces as they spun on a ride or dipped down the glistening rollercoaster tracks, painted faces on the posters advertising "the greatest collection of freaks ever assembled under one tent!"

Even Diane's and Jenny's faces seemed somehow unreal. They were in conversation, but Patty had trouble focusing on their words. Only their faces were clear—Diane's so cynical; Jenny's so too-fresh, too-open. Funny how two people the same age and with relatively the same background could be so different.

Diane was a beautiful girl, Patty thought. One of those people on whom cynicism looks attractive. She looked older than her nineteen years and implied by her style that she had lived twice that long. You got the impression that if anyone knew what was wrong with something, Diane did. And it was always Diane who spoke up when someone was trying to take advantage or when the group was undecided as to whether to attempt something risky. Diane was good to have as a friend and dangerous to have as an enemy.

Jenny, on the other hand, was a follower. She never initiated, not because she did not have a mind of her own, but because of a kind of timidity that everyone else thought was cute. Perhaps that was why she maintained it.

Patty could not help wondering what *she* looked like as she tried to join the conversation.

Diane was laughing, "So I kinda look him over, see, and I mean he must have been straight from the farm! He starts blushing! I mean he was really looking miserable. I'll bet that preacher really thought he was getting through!" And she laughed again.

"What do you think about what he said?" Jenny asked, with what seemed more than idle curiosity.

"What *who* said?" Diane was still enjoying her little triumph.

"The guy who was preaching. The singer."

"I think it was all a bunch of—" Diane's description was lost in the shouts of two little boys chasing a runaway balloon.

Patty was finally with the conversation. "Some people get all strung out on things that don't matter," she injected. "*I'm* a Christian."

Jenny's eyes became even rounder. "You are?"

"Oh, not like *he* was pushing. I go to church just about every week. I try to follow the Ten Commandments. I believe in God, and I try to help people."

Diane put her hand on Patty's head and entoned, "My dear, you are practically a missionary!" And the two laughed.

Jenny was quiet.

15

"I mean, what else is there, really?" Patty said with finality, not expecting an answer.

"I—I don't know," Jenny said, almost to herself.

"Come on, friends," Diane said with new enthusiasm. "Let the dead bury the dead. I think that's in the Bible, isn't it? Let's go on some rides."

"Good idea," Patty answered, glad to shake the final words of the singer from her mind.

"You go ahead," Jenny said, quite out of character for one who usually followed. "Maybe I'll go back to that tent and hear a little more of what he has to say."

"Oh, brother," Diane said, rolling her eyes heavenward. "Look, I paid a bundle for these ride tickets, and I'm going to use them. You can always get converted later—free!"

* * *

"That's right, Jenny, in a way it is free. What I mean is, it doesn't cost you anything but your life."

Jenny sat at a small table in the tent. The music now came from a tape and was background to conversations taking place at similar tables around the canvas room. A quiet, pretty girl who appeared to be in her mid-twenties was talking with Jenny. The badge that she was wearing identified her as a counselor named Sally.

"That sounds pretty expensive," Jenny answered. It was not a quip. It was a thoughtful response to the idea that being saved also meant giving up your life.

"It might seem that way until you realize that you're letting God, who created you—the God who

16

cares for you more than any human ever could—that you're letting Him take over." And then she added with a grin, "There's no way you can lose."

Jenny was not used to making decisions, especially radical ones. And this was a radical decision. The gospel was making sense to her. She had never heard it presented so simply. She had to agree that she was selfish—even she, who always went along with everything everyone *else* wanted to do. She knew somehow more clearly now than she had ever seen it that her agreeableness was only designed to *get* affection from others.

She saw that, when faced with the responsibility of living a life worthy of the holy God who had put her on His earth, she was short of the mark. Maybe she had not committed any of the gross sins, but, as Sally had said, "How many sins does it take to be a sinner?" Jenny knew that she had committed probably the grossest sin of all, that of ignoring her Creator. She found herself struggling inside in a way that was unfamiliar to her. The sounds of the fair began reaching out for her attention, offering to take her away from the struggle.

* * *

Outside the tent, and not too far away, Diane and Patty were having troubles of their own. Patty was on her hands and knees, pushing aside some tall grass that edged a tent.

"I had them a minute ago," she said. "They must

17

have dropped out of my purse when I got my brush. What are we going to do?"

Diane did not have a chance to answer.

"Troubles?" A young, masculine voice entered their scene. Two boys were standing there, giving the incident the look of a magazine novel. They were both sturdy, good looking, and obviously interested in getting to know Patty and Diane.

Diane was delighted and did not mind showing it. "Hello," she said, but with that rising and falling inflection that says, "You're more than welcome."

Patty was embarrassed at being on all fours. "Oh, I just lost my tickets."

"I've got a whole pocket full," one of the boys said as he offered her a hand to stand up.

"Oh, I couldn't—" she began to answer, but Diane was louder.

"Oh, yes you *could*! Otherwise, you'll be using mine all afternoon!"

"Maybe you won't need them," the other boy spoke up. "I'm Jerry."

"I'm Patty."

"I'm Jim."

"I'm Diane, and I'm just dying to get up on that ferris wheel!" She was never one to miss the last word.

They all laughed and coupled off—Patty and Jim, Diane and Jerry—to line up for the big wheel.

* * *

Jenny was turning over in her mind what she was hearing. Sally was not pushy, but she seemed to know the objections Jenny thought of before she could verbalize them.

"Going to church, trying to follow the commandments—all that is okay, Jenny, but you can't confuse that with true Christianity."

Jenny could hear Patty's words, "I'm a Christian. I go to church. I try to follow—"

"You see, the Bible tells us what we already know about ourselves; we just can't be perfect. And yet our God *is* a perfect, *holy* God. There is just no way in His present state and ours for us to get together. But He's done it for us. That's why He came to earth. Jesus Christ was born a human being. And He grew and lived the very life God's holiness demands of each of us. He did it for us! And then—then He was punished and killed. He was punished as though He

19

was one of us. He *lived* in our place, and then He *died* in our place."

Jenny saw, for the first time clearly, what the word "sacrifice" really meant. Bits and pieces of past Easter programs and paintings and sculptures passed through her mind. She began to see the man, Jesus, as actually having lived and died. And He had died in her place.

"It seems—it seems so unfair," she stammered.

"Whoever said love was fair?" came the quiet, simple reply. "When you begin to see just how far God has gone to bring us back to Himself, you begin to see what the real meaning of love is."

Again, Jenny was in turmoil. What if this God whom she had ignored, sometimes avoided consciously, had really done all this for her? Again the sounds of the fair tried to jam her thoughts.

* * *

"I love it! I just love it!" Diane was shouting as the four of them climbed into one of the helicopters which was available at five dollars per head per ride.

"Stick with me, baby," Jerry was doing what he called his Humphrey Pushcart imitation, "and you'll understand what the meanin' of flyin' really is!"

"Aren't you just a little scared?" Patty asked Jim, as they were being strapped into their seats.

"I've never heard of them leaving anyone up there."

* * *

The folds in the roof of the tent where the canvas

20

converged with the center pole looked to Jenny like some great complex arrow pointing up. They could have been all the many trails she had followed in her not totally conscious search for meaning. And here, in this tent ("trap," Diane had called it), everything in her was looking up.

"He came back to life, Jenny," Sally was saying. "This is probably the most difficult part of the whole story, and the most important. Jesus came back to life and still actually lives today! We're not talking about applying some good principles that a dead someone laid out a few thousand years ago. We're talking about asking a very alive God to apply His sacrificial death to your account, freeing you from absolutely all guilt. And then we're asking that same *living* Jesus to show Himself alive to you personally. Ask Him to enter your life, Jenny. He will."

No one makes the decision easily. Not when they really consider the truth of it. God becomes human? And dies as a sacrifice rather than striking His insubordinate creatures dead themselves? And then returns to life and actually invades the lives of those who open themselves to Him? A God who waits politely for an invitation? No one makes the decision easily. Because it really does cost the believer his whole life. He has to accept as true a story more impossible than anything man's imagination could come up with. He has to speak in prayer as though there is Someone who listens and answers. He has to open his life to the possibility of an actual supernatural existence somehow moving in and sharing

21

space. It is a radical move. No one makes the decision easily.

And Jenny's stumbling prayer was not easy. At first the words came, separated by long pauses, as though she were listening to see how far they were traveling. "O God, I know I've spent a long time of my life just doing what I wanted to do. I haven't given much—any—thought to what You wanted."

But as the prayer continued, a change was taking place in Jenny. She was becoming progressively less self-conscious and obviously more conscious of something—Someone—else. "And yet, You have done—given—everything for me. You gave Your life for me. If I—if I were the only person on earth, You would have done it just for me—just so my sins would be forgiven. And You say You'll come now and live in my heart. I—I want that, dear God. Oh, I want that! I want to be forgiven, and I want You to live in me. Take my life, dear God."

By now Jenny's tone and expression were totally changed. Smiles, almost laughs, began interrupting her words. "Oh, Lord—Lord—thank You. Oh, thank You."

"That was a beautiful prayer, Jenny. I know the Lord will honor it."

"He has! He already has!" The tears running down her cheeks only made her new glow sparkle. "I feel it! I feel *Him*! I feel like—like if I had wings, I could fly! Right up to Him!"

"You don't need wings, Jenny. You don't need wings."

TWO

Whap! Patty smacked the rolled-up magazine against the screen door. She killed the fly, but some of its sticky remains clung to the magazine in her hand. Patty had been bothered by the fly when it was alive; now she was even more disgusted with it. She looked around the room for something to clean both the screen and the magazine, and finally simply dropped the periodical, plop, into a nearby wastebasket.

Patty smiled at the contrast between the mess she had just dropped in and the sign on the wastebasket itself. It read, "Conrad's Solid Comfort Camps," and it matched the print on her sweatshirt.

Conrad's was the one place in town, or just outside town, where there was always summer work for old friends; and Patty, Jenny, Diane, and many others had been working there since early high school. Conrad himself was nonexistent, or so the rumor was. His name was painted over entrances to trailer camps all across the contry, but no one recalled ever actually having seen even a picture of him. On rainy days when the miniature golf course and the pool

23

and ping pong tables were vacant and there was not much to do with the grounds, the summer staff would sit around the pop machine and fabricate long, involved stories as to Conrad's real identity and current whereabouts. He was always somewhere in "solid comfort."

Patty smiled. She began to think of her recent victim as being named Conrad. He had been in disguise, and—

"Do you have the extra key for the miniature golf equipment?" Jenny's voice broke into Patty's story.

"No. Sorry," Patty answered, squinting slightly, as the light coming from behind Jenny through the screen door momentarily overpowered her vision. "Diane took mine."

"Well, that's that, I guess."

"What do you mean? She should be right back."

"Have you seen the new lifeguard at the pool?"

"No."

"Well, Diane *has*!"

"Oh," Patty answered, knowing full well what that meant. The key in question might very well be sitting at the bottom of the pool, having "accidentally" dropped out of Diane's hand, and "Could you be a sweetie and just go down there and get it for me?" And of course he would, and a whole new thing would be begun.

Jenny nodded in agreement. The story she was imagining for Diane might not have been exactly the same, but the general outline and climax was always the same, and it was that to which she was nodding.

24

"That really surprises me," Patty finally said. "I thought that guy we met at the fair really got to her. You know—Jerry?"

"I didn't meet him."

"Oh, that's right. You went back to that tent. Hey, could you come in here? I can hardly see you with all that light blasting in from over your shoulder."

"Oh, sure. Sorry." Jenny said, and stepped in.

Patty had another of her strange visions—like the faces that afternoon at the fair. For just a second it looked as though Jenny brought the light into the room with her. It was only a flash, but it startled Patty. She moved the conversation along, pushing away the strange feeling. "Too bad you missed them. We met a couple of really groovy guys."

"I—I met Jesus," Jenny responded quietly. She had been wanting to share her new experience of Jesus with her friends but had not known where to start. This morning she had said, as she prayed, "Today, Lord. With Patty or Diane, or with somebody else. But today." And here she was, saying something that sounded so simple as to be stupid.

Patty either didn't know what to say or really hadn't heard her. "What?"

Jenny dug her toes into her thongs and started again. "I met Jesus—Christ. I know what Dave—the singer—was talking about. Because I—I'm a Christian now."

And there it was, plain and simple. Jenny waited, not knowing what to expect. She had never talked to anyone like that before. But whatever she had expected, it did not happen. Patty was obviously puzzled by what she had just heard. But Patty was also a longtime friend.

"Well, that's—that's great, Jenny," Patty said with a certain amount of enthusiasm. "I hope it works out well for you."

* * *

"I felt so stupidly stupid!" Jenny said, and hit the golf ball at such an angle that it careened off the side, the back, and the other side of the miniature green, and came to rest just inches from where it had started. "Just like that!" Jenny said, more emotionally involved with the game than she had ever been.

Her two partners laughed the kind of laugh that is designed to ease someone's frustration. Sally, the girl who had been sharing Jesus with her when she had given herself to Him, and Dave, the singer from the group in the tent, had joined Jenny at Conrad's for a night game of golf and talk.

"That wasn't a wasted shot, Jenny," Dave was saying. "To you, maybe, it seemed stupid. Okay, so you didn't spell out the whole gospel, the theology of the Trinity, and a defined eschatology—"

"I didn't what?" Jenny asked, trying to follow Dave's thought.

Sally and Dave laughed again. "What the learned reverend is trying to say, Jenny," Sally chimed in, "is that in some ways what you said was *better* than a well-footnoted, canned speech. What you said was what you knew to be true."

26

"It was like baby talk!"

"But it was *true*, Jenny, and *that's* what's important. So many Christians spend long hours planning out their testimony; and when they get done, it's lost all its vitality, its living truth. It turns out to be just a group of well-chosen phrases that anyone with any grasp of the language could put together. People are looking for *life* and *truth* these days, Jenny. Not just fancier phrases. *Anybody* can convey the Christian *message*, whether they believe it or not. Actors do it all the time. So do a lot of phonies. Our job as Christians is to convey the Christian *life*. And it doesn't take a second look," Dave added with a warm smile, "to see that Jesus really is alive in you."

It was a strangely warm moment for Jenny. She wanted to feel embarrassed—look down, or something that seemed the proper humble thing to do. But she knew that what Dave had said was true. Jesus really was living in her. And she was noticeably different. She knew that. Her parents had mentioned it. Even her little sister had asked her what had happened. And so to act embarrassed would be to disclaim what was true, and she could not do that. Jesus had done, and was doing, beautiful things inside.

She smiled and said quietly, "Praise God."

"Jenny!" Patty's voice came from the darkened buildings a short way from the lighted course. And soon Patty appeared, still in her Conrad's uniform, but with her purse across her shoulder.

"You're working late." Jenny smiled at her.

27

"A little. I'm on my way home now. Glad I caught you people together."

"This is Sally and Dave," Jenny began introductions. "I met them at the tent—"

But Patty was farther along in her thought. "I recognized the singer. Nice to meet you. Listen, Jim—the guy *I* met at the fair—and I are throwing a little water skiing and picnic thing on Saturday afternoon out at the dam. We're asking everybody."

"Sounds great," Dave answered immediately.

"It really does," Sally added, "but I'm afraid I've got other plans. Thanks."

"Oh, that's too bad," Jenny said.

"How about you?" Patty asked, with a gesture toward Dave. "You have other plans?"

"Not that I know of," he answered.

"Well, why don't *you* take *her*?" and Patty's gesture moved from Dave to Jenny. Then she suddenly dropped it. "Unless you and Sally have something going."

"No," Dave said almost too quickly. "I mean, yes, I'd like to. I mean, it's okay with me."

"Good," Patty clipped. "You can even bring your guitar if you want to."

* * *

"You know, Jenny," Diane was sprawled out on a blanket in the Saturday afternoon shade, "your boyfriend isn't a bad guy for a preacher."

"He's not my boyfriend, and he's not a preacher," Jenny said simply.

Diane raised up on one hand. "But he *is* the guy

who was at the fair making all that scarey talk about the end of the world and all that, isn't he?''

"That's just something Christians believe.''

"Do *you* believe all that?''

"I don't know enough about it.''

Diane stretched out again on the blanket, and all three girls watched the clouds changing color and texture as the sun dropped lower and lower in the sky.

The afternoon had been all action and laughs. Each in turn had gotten up on the skis, and each in

turn had been dumped, many times. Jim and Patty had tried some two-on-the-skis maneuvering; and although they would certainly never be the featured performers at a water ballet, they got to like what they were doing together more and more.

Dave had played his guitar during most of the eating, and he surprised a few there by knowing more than just old standards and religious songs.

Jerry had come with Diane. No one asked what happened to the new lifeguard. And Jerry was funny. He had a new voice and a funny line for just about every situation. Jim did not laugh as much at Jerry as the others did, but then he had heard the voices and the lines many times before. Every time, in fact, that a new audience gathered.

Now the skiing and the food and the sunlight was almost gone, and the boys had gone in search of wood for a fire. Patty, Diane, and Jenny lazed, and long pauses fell in between their sentences.

"How's *your* new guy working out?" Diane finally said, rolling slightly toward Patty.

Patty smiled for a long time, as though she were trying to play one of Diane's games of suggestion and intrigue. But she could not handle it. She had to say, "Oh, just great! I really like him."

Diane was up on one arm again. "Well, if you really want to keep him, my child, maybe it's time I taught you a few of the facts—of—life." The smile that crept across her face foretold just how biological her facts of life were going to be.

Jenny stood up and started to walk away.

Diane was not satisfied to let it go. "Where are you going?"

"Just—just for a little walk," Jenny answered. It was obvious that Jenny did not want to make an issue, but Diane did. In the past, half the fun for Diane was watching Jenny's eyes grow bigger and rounder as she told of her many exploits in dark places. Now the new Jenny was walking out.

"Why don't you stick around, kid? You might learn something."

It was a sad smile that came to Jenny's face. It might have been mild pity. "I'm sorry, Diane. I just don't want to hear that kind of talk."

In the uncomfortable pause that followed, Patty found herself looking at faces again. She saw the face of her wise friend, Diane, who was in the process of finding a remark which would recover her stronger position in the discussion. Jenny's reproof had been mild but effective. And there was Jenny's face, again hard to see because the late afternoon sun was coming from behind her. Patty wondered if the light would always be coming from Jenny from now on. It was silly thought.

Diane was finally ready with her retort. "Well, maybe we'll have our little talk later—after the *children* go to bed." The word *children* was punched a little too hard even for Diane. It indicated just how put down she felt. And then, without allowing breathing or rebuttal space, she launched into a new conversation with Patty. "Did you tell me your guy was working in a zoo?"

31

"Not in a zoo! At a zoo. He's studying to be a veterinarian, so it's a good deal for the summer."

"That's wild. Jerry's pre-med. We got ourselves a couple of doctors!" Diane laughed heartily, as did Patty. Jenny stood, listening, then sat down on the blanket, and waited to be included in the conversation. The incident was soon forgotten.

"What's Jerry doing this summer?" Patty asked, glad the emotional clouds had blown away.

"He's working in his own kind of zoo. He's an ambulance attendant."

"Yech!"

"That's what I said. Jerry says it does get a little gory once in a while, but a lot of the time he just sits around waiting to be called. He says you never know when it's going to happen, day or night."

*   *   *

"No one knows when it's going to happen," Dave was saying. The boys had returned, and a small fire glowed near the group. It was much later, now, and the highs of the day were settling like the coals. The six looked into the embers as Dave continued. "And when they asked Him, Jesus said even He didn't know the exact time. But it is going to happen. One of these days—could be any minute now—Jesus will come back for His own. And after that, it'll be pretty awful here on earth."

"Like what?" Jim asked without looking away from the fire. He and Patty were leaning against each other in a lazy, comfortable way. She glanced up at his face, surprised to hear his voice as quiet and thoughtful as the question had come out.

"Well, for example, the Bible says that right now the Spirit of God is holding back the full power of evil in the world. But when the believers go, the Spirit will go, too. That means a whole new ball game, only this time with no rules. Evil will just take over, and the evil one—the Bible calls him the Antichrist, the Beast—will reign supreme."

Somehow, words like this were strong said into the fire, Patty thought. You could almost believe the stuff he was saying. But she also knew that in the brightness of a new day, it would all return to the superstition bag.

"See, we just don't know what it would be like to live in a world like that. The good around us still has the support of the Spirit of God. But when He goes—wow!"

"You really believe all that?" Jerry asked. It was one of those rare occasions when he used his own voice.

"Of course," Dave answered simply.

And Jerry was back, this time with a broad Chinese attempt. "Ah-rots-ah-ruck!"

A light chuckle passed around, but Dave quietly ended it with, "I'll tell you this, those who are left here will *need* it."

A feeling of uncomfortableness moved around the group, although no one looked up. Each sat with his thoughts for a few minutes. Dave hoped that what he was saying was really getting through. *Spirit of God,* he prayed within himself, *all I can do is tell them. You have to make them believe.*

Jenny's feelings were mixed. It had not been that long since she had considered a person's religion his own business—his own choice. Now she realized that settling things with God was as important—was *more* important than any other act if life. It was no more "you believe your way and I'll believe mine." It was "Please, you must understand. This is important. This is life or death—forever!" She sat, squirming. But as soon as she realized that she was moving, she stopped, fearing it might distract from what Dave had been saying.

Jerry and Diane looked into the fire, both with half-smiles on their faces. The single source of light and their similar expressions made them look somehow alike. But although their faces were still, their hands were not. They were finding each other in the dark, and their thoughts were far from the conversation.

Patty, on the other hand, felt strangely creepy. She did not want to believe what Dave had been saying, but there was enough superstitious belief in her that the Bible was somehow true to add weight to his words. Some of her said, "This is frightening. What should I do?" But some of her said "Sure, it's scary. But when he stops talking about it, it will go away; and everything will be all right again."

Patty momentarily lost her balance as Jim sat more upright. He was focused tightly on the conversation. "If you really believed all that," he started, slowly, "you couldn't even look at your watch without wondering if it were going to happen—now!"

Patty shuddered. She pulled her sweater closer to her, hoping to hide the fact that her shudder was not from cold.

"That's right," Dave answered. Then he smiled, "But to the Christian, it's something we look forward to. The non-Christian is waiting for the end of life. Doom. The believer is waiting to meet the One who *gave* him life."

Perhaps it was Jim's intense interest, but Patty found herself more involved. "Is that beast you talk about the same one who's supposed to go around marking people?" she asked. "My grandmother told me about the terrible things that are supposed to happen."

"The mark of the beast is talked about," Dave said quietly. "It's probably some kind of identification mark based on the number 666. The Bible says that people won't be able to buy or sell without it. Kind of a super-evil credit card, only you'll wear it on your hand or your forehead."

Diane's voice was low and sultry. "I wouldn't let anyone tattoo my forehead."

And again, Dave had a quiet comeback. "You don't even have to be around when it happens."

The group sat quietly again, staring at the remaining embers. Now and then the area received a brief splash of light as a car drove over the dam above. The sound of the water surging through the two open gates in the dam seemed to rise as they sat

35

silent. There was some light in the night sky, perhaps from the moon, but its source was not seen from where they sat.

Then suddenly, abruptly, there was a violent movement in the dark. Diane shrieked in surprise. A dark figure was standing between them and the dying fire.

"Yes you do, baby." The voice that came from the figure was Jerry's "Humphrey Pushcart." He had suddenly leapt to his feet and was facing them in the dark.

Diane laughed in relief. "Do I?"

"That's right, sweetheart. Because I like you. Can't you see that?"

"I kinda got the idea," Diane said, still laughing. "But what's that got to do with my being around when the tattooing starts?"

"Because, baby, *I am* the Antichrist!"

Patty shuddered again, and this time Jim put an arm around her in an almost comforting move. Diane roared with laughter and then said in long, low tones, "Good. I always was a sucker for beasts!"

THREE

"I'm not sure air conditioning would even help," Patty thought to herself as she sat in church the following morning. The day before, she had heard things that she had been told were in the Bible. Things that bothered her sleep. But here she was, in her usual spot on Sunday morning, trying to be interested in what the minister was saying.

"When one brings to a discussion of this kind, plain old—and I might add God-given—common sense, one sees immediately that those differences which men of old deemed worthy of death, are really dead horses."

Patty idly reached for the Bible next to the hymnal in the rack in front of her and began flipping through it. She had no idea where to look for anything, but Saturday had not worn off. "Of the children of Naphtali, throughout their generations, after their families, by the house of their fathers, according to the number of the names, from twenty years old and upward—"*

* Numbers 1:42, King James Version

37

Who could understand any of it? Patty thought, and closed the book.

"Ask yourself the simplest of questions," the Reverend Mr. Turner continued to those who were still awake enough to ask the simplest of questions. "Do these so-called basic tenets of Christianity really affect me at all? Would I appreciate beauty any less if Jesus were not virgin born? Would I respect the rights of others less if He had not gone about the countryside performing miracles? Could I really be considered so gross as to somehow be responsible for the death of the Son of God?"

And yet, Patty was thinking again, *what Dave was quoting from the Bible didn't seem all that obscure.* She opened the Bible again.

The minister was unaware of Patty's lack of interest. "I would not be so harsh as to condemn humanity to a fiery pit; can I be more merciful than God, who, it is reported, is love? You can see where you are led by such simple, obvious questions. To insist that the Bible is anything but the poetic expression of the greater principles by which man lives with man, is to box yourself in with a wealth of opinion and counteropinion which, in the long run, doesn't really matter because it really doesn't affect the way you are."

"He came unto his own, and his own received him not. But as many as received him, to them gave he power to become the sons of God, even to them that believe on his name: which were born, not of blood, nor of the will of the flesh, nor of the will of man, but

38

of God."* Patty closed the book again. At least she understood the words. But it was all so remote. So other-worldly. Why should religion be so hard to grasp?

"What matters, my friends, is what we *can* know about. Man's relation to man! Create the universe in six days if you like, but don't force this myth on me as fact. Don't make our relationship depend on my accepting it! Believe in a literal Adam, believe in a literal Eve, have a literal garden and snake, if you like—"

*   *   *

It was a real snake that discovered the open pen door at the zoo later that afternoon. Jim was preparing to crate the cobra for shipping and had

* John 1: 11-13

39

left the pen door ajar while he made a few adjustments on the shipping crate. His attention was on his work, and the cobra slid silently out beside him.

Jim stopped hammering to wipe the perspiration from his face. He looked up at the open, blue sky and thought about how nice it might be to be sprawled out under a tree with something cool to drink and Patty to look at. His mind went to the day before, and some of what Dave had been talking about. He looked at his watch, and remembered, *"If you believed that, you couldn't look at your watch—"*

He shook his head, took another tack from the many sticking out of his mouth, and began hammering it into place.

The cobra had discovered Jim and was watching him while it quietly curled into a solid mass and raised its head.

But is that a good enough reason to buy a guy's religion? Jim thought. *Fear that you might be left behind? I don't know. I don't like scare tactics in any kind of selling pitch, and religion is no different. Still, I can't just rule it out without finding—*

That was the end of Jim's thought. A sudden, sharp pain in his leg, a turn to see, a realization of what had hit him, a few feeble shouts for help, and everything grew dizzily, fuzzily gray.

"Now, you just kinda hang in there, son," the voice blurred in Jim's consciousness, but it sounded like Jerry's attempt at Jimmy Stewart. "We've got the best doctors in the country lined up and twiddlin' their thumbs, waitin' till you get there."

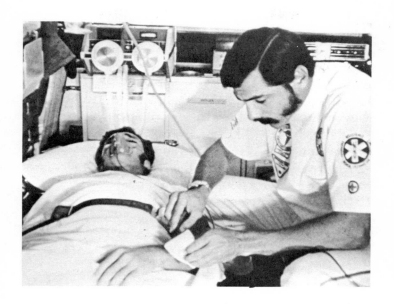

It was Jerry, and his voice was only an attempt. He had seen enough people in the back of the ambulance to know that Jim was really in trouble. And he did not have a ready funny line for a friend who was on his way out from a cobra bite.

*   *   *

I'm sorry, but there are no visitors allowed in there at the moment," the nurse told Patty and Jenny as they leaned over the counter of the nurses' station in the emergency ward.

"But he's my—" Patty did not exactly know what to call Jim. She knew that he had become, in a very short time, very dear to her. So dear, in fact, that when Diane had called after Jerry had called her, and told of Jim's accident, she had done two unusual things. First she had called Jenny. There was something somehow right about the way Jenny was with God that made her the person to call on at a time like this. And second, she had rushed to the hospital just to—she did not know what. "Why won't they let me see him?" Patty was pacing in anguish.

"You heard what they said," Jenny answered, sympathetically. "No one is allowed—"

"I know, I know! Don't they have any feelings in this dump? If I could just find out how he—"

The door to the room the nurse had gestured toward opened, and a small, balding man came out, a worried look on his face. Patty ran to him.

"Is Jim Wright in that room?" She nearly shouted.

The man was startled out of his thoughts. "I beg your pardon?"

"Jim Wright. We're friends of his, and we just—"

"I'm afraid you won't be able to see him just now. We're pretty busy."

"I know that. I just want to know how he is. Will he be all right?" Patty was struggling to sound in control. The little man may have been a doctor, but he did not have about him a professional, confidence-producing look. He seemed preoccupied, worried, and, Patty thought, not quite with it.

"Yes, well, it really wouldn't be fair for me to evaluate the situation at this minute. I mean, not that snake bites are unusual. Happen all the time. But not so much around here. And he was bitten by a large Indian cobra. Now, that's serious business, and

42

we're doing everything we can to get help here for him."

"To get help *here*?" Patty shrieked, and Jenny touched her arm. "What do you mean? Isn't there anyone here who can help him? What kind of help? How long will it take?"

"Now, perhaps you'd better just sit down, young lady. You're upset."

"I'm fine," Patty yelled, drawing the attention of everyone in the halls in all directions. Then, realizing how she sounded, she dropped her volume, and spoke, one careful word at a time, as though speaking to someone who understood very little English. "I am his friend. I am concerned about him. Please tell me what you meant when you said you were getting help here for him."

"We've sent for a man in Florida who runs a snake farm. Over the years his blood has built up antibodies needed to fight the kind of poison in your friend's system. There is no serum to handle it, so we're hoping a blood transfusion from this man will provide the antidote."

*   *   *

"How fast does this thing fly?" the large, bearded man in the jean suit shouted over the roar of the engine as they lifted off the small Florida airstrip.

"About 230 miles per hour if the winds are right."

The bearded passenger looked at his watch and sat back, trying to relax. It would be a few hours before he could help—if he could help. Had he been a praying man, he might have spent the time with

43

God. But he was forced to just sit and wait, as the ground moved seemingly slowly beneath the plane.

* * *

Back at the hospital, Jenny was praying. "Dear Lord, You say in Your Word that everything works out for the best to those who love You. Well, Jim doesn't exactly love You—yet—but I think there's a good chance he will. He seems really interested when we talk. Oh, Lord, let Jim make it, if it is Your will. You know what the reason is behind this crisis. Give us faith. Use it, and give us the courage to accept Your will. Please, Lord, let that man get here in time to save Jim. In Jesus' name. Amen."

Patty stopped pacing in front of Jenny. The three hours they had been in the waiting room were showing. "What about me?" she snapped, and then, surprised at the sharpness of her own voice, she apologized. "I'm sorry, Jenny. I didn't mean—"

"That's okay," Jenny answered quietly. "What *did* you mean?"

"I guess—I guess when I heard you praying for Jim the way you did—like the only reason for him to stay alive was so that he could believe in God, or something—I guess I just wanted you to ask God to keep him alive for *me*. I know that sounds foolish. I—"

"I don't think it sounds foolish, Patty. Really, I don't. If I felt about Jim the way you do, I'd want the same thing."

Patty was quieted by Jenny's words, and sat next to her on the bench.

44

"In one way," Jenny continued, quietly, "if Jim *were* a Christian, it wouldn't matter so much."

"I—I just can't see it, Jenny. It's no good trying to preach to me now. I'm too upset."

There was renewed activity in and out of the room in which Jim lay. "Has he arrived?" Patty asked a young orderly as he hurried out of the room.

"Who? Oh, the snake bite guy? No. Not yet."

"Then what's all the—"

"He's starting to get paralyzed. He's starting to drown in his own spit. They're getting the—" But his explanation was cut short by a quiet but stern order from someone inside the room, and the orderly hurried off.

"Drown?" Patty's voice was cracked with emotion. "Paralyzed?"

"Please wait in the waiting area," a nurse demanded, as she and another orderly wheeled some machinery that appeared to be all tubing into the room. And before Patty could say anything, the door was closed.

Jenny did not say anything. There was nothing to say. She took Patty's arm gently, and led her back to the waiting area. Patty followed, too stunned by the thoughts crowding her mind to know where she was going. Jenny sat down and said, "Patty, try to stay right here. Please. Don't go away. I want to make a phone call. All right?"

Patty nodded, slowly, uttering something like "Right." She stared ahead, looking at the pictures in her mind, rather than at the room around her.

Jenny walked a few steps away, tentatively, looked

back, and seeing that Patty was not going anywhere, ran to the pay phone just outside the waiting room door.

"I'll be right over," Pastor Ed Belevedere said, and hung up the phone. He stood in his study, and was about to rush out, when his eyes caught the small sign he had hung just below the sheepskins which showed him a master of both theology and psychology. His sign read, "Tell Jesus," and had served as a reminder many times that his real availability was to the Lord.

Pastor Belevedere sat again, and said, "Lord, thank You for tapping me on the shoulder. I have no idea what I can do for that boy in the hospital. I don't know what Jenny expects, or what her friend Patty needs. But You know the whole situation, and You have called me into it. Please, Lord, free me from anything that would hinder the flow of Your Holy Spirit in this situation. I go only as Your representative, and claim the power of Your name. Amen."

Then, picking up his Bible, he hurried from the church.

* * *

"It won't be long now," the pilot of the small plane shouted to his passenger. "They're holding all other traffic to get us in, and there's a police escort waiting at the airport. If you don't get there in time, it sure won't be because we didn't try."

His bearded passenger forced a smile in response. He knew the agonies of snake bite, and had given some hurried insights over the phone at home before he had raced to the airport. Checking his watch, he

46

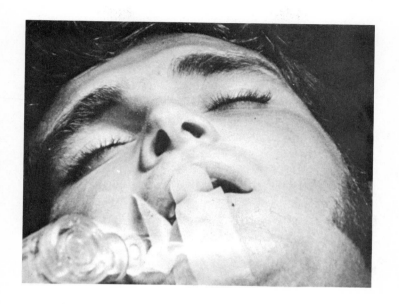

knew that the young patient he was hoping to help would be in great pain, eased only by cutting in and out of consciousness. "I hope he's in good physical condition," he muttered to himself.

* * *

"Lord, we don't know what You have in mind for this boy, but we commit this situation into Your hands." Pastor Belevedere was standing beside the bed where Jim lay, attached to a number of machines. It was obvious that each machine was active, and that together they were sustaining his life. "And we pray that Your expressed will is done. We would ask, dear heavenly Father, that this boy be given another opportunity to commit his life to You.

47

We pray for the speed of the man who is coming to help. And we ask all in the name of Jesus Christ, our Lord. Amen."

As soon as the prayer ended, an impatient nurse hurried the pastor out of the room. He was met immediately by an impatient Patty. "How is he?"

"It's hard to tell. They've got him hooked up to a lot of sophisticated machinery."

"You've seen lots of people in hospitals. What's he look like?"

"Well, I'm afraid I haven't the medical knowledge to give you anything but a guess, Patty. But I'd say they're doing everything possible. Why don't we just sit and wait for a while?"

As he said this, Pastor Belevedere led Patty back to the bench where Jenny waited.

"Why does everybody keep bringing me to this bench?" Patty shouted.

There was a small, embarrassed pause. Then the pastor spoke. "She's right, Jenny. Why don't we all go downstairs to the coffee shop and have something? I'll tell the nurse where we'll be. We're not doing Jim or anybody any good getting in the way up here."

The coffee shop was a welcome change for Patty, even though she felt too far away from Jim. She barely tasted the doughnut or the coffee, and she barely heard the conversation Jenny and the pastor were trying to engage her in. But she seemed to hear every siren that approached the hospital; every squeal of brakes.

48

What she did not know was that one siren and one squeal belonged to a police car rather than an ambulance. And before the squeal stopped, a bearded man in a jean suit was running toward an elevator, in the company of three white-jacketed men.

Patty looked at the clock, and then jumped to her feet. "We've been here almost an hour!" she said, and started walking through the cluster of tables and chairs toward the elevator, Jenny and the pastor following close behind.

But she was stopped when the elevator door slid open, and the doctor came out. "Oh, there you are," he said, with no discernable show of emotion on his face.

A quick look passed between Jenny and the pastor which seemed to say, "Be ready to handle anything she might do when she hears the news." They moved closer to her.

"Is he—" Patty could not find the words to finish her sentence.

"He'll be okay," the doctor said, and something of a smile came to his face.

"Thank You, Lord," Jenny breathed.

"Praise God," Pastor Belevedere echoed.

"Yes, well we all worked very hard," the doctor added awkwardly.

It was only an hour later when Patty was told that Jim was conscious and could be seen. She almost ran to the door, but as she reached the room, she was suddenly struck with the fact that she really did not know Jim very well; that she was not even sure how he felt about her; that it may have been a totally one-sided situation. They had had terrific times when they were together, and had exchanged many of their closest thoughts. But she was not sure.

As she walked quietly into the room, Jim stirred, and his eyes turned toward her. He smiled a tired smile that had warmth.

"How—how are you?" Patty asked, not knowing what to say.

"I haven't felt this bad," Jim half whispered, "since I ate my sister's first casserole."

It was not that funny, but it was enough to release the tension Patty had stored up the past hours. She laughed, and tears spilled out of her eyes.

Instinctively, she put her hand on his, and Jim's fingers curled around hers. His grip was weak, but it was steady.

"I'm glad—I'm glad you're okay. I really am," she said, brushing the tears away with her free hand.

"You know," Jim whispered, "there's a lot—I mean, you and me. I—"

That was all Patty needed. Just that much. "We'll talk when you're feeling better." She smiled, and the tears flowed again.

They looked at each other in silence for a long time. Occasionally, Patty brushed away more tears, sniffed, and laughed a little embarrassed laugh, but most of the time they just looked. And the room seemed to be filled with the words, "I love you! I love you!"

FOUR

"Jim!" Jenny's eyes sparkled with surprise as she stopped on the steps leading to the church sanctuary. It had been only a few weeks since the hospital vigil, and Jenny had not seen him since his release.

She hurried over to him, her sister, Susan, at her elbow. "How are you feeling? I'm so glad to see you."

"A lot better, thanks. Patty told me about how you helped while I was—"

"Is Patty here?" Jenny asked, looking around.

"No. She doesn't even know *I'm* here."

Susan cleared her throat, obviously to remind Jenny that her sister was waiting to be introduced.

"Oh, I'm sorry, honey," Jenny said, getting the implication. "Jim, this is my sister, Sue. Sue, Jim Wright."

"Are you the one who got bit by the cobra?" Susan launched out.

"I'm the one," Jim said, with a light celebrity bounce in his manner.

"Wow!" And that was all Sue could think of to

say. She looked at him with eleven-year-old marvel, and then said it again. "Wow!"

Jim was again talking with Jenny. "Frankly, I don't even know why I came here his morning. We were driving by yesterday, and Patty pointed out your church and said something about your pastor having come to pray for me while I was—you know—bad, and—well, here I am."

"We're really glad to have you, Jim. Do you remember Pastor Belevedere praying?"

"A little, I guess. It's all fuzzy, but I remember that after he left, I felt a kind of strange peace about everything. Like I somehow knew I was going to make it. I can't explain it exactly, and I just don't know what to think of the things I've been feeling ever since."

Jenny's face shone with a brilliant smile. "You came to the right place to find out, Jim."

* * *

"Now, it says in First Thessalonians, chapter five, verse one, 'When is all this going to happen? I really don't need to say anything about that, dear brothers, for you know perfectly well that no one knows. That day of the Lord will come unexpectedly like a thief in the night. When people are saying, 'All is well, everything is quiet and peaceful'—then, all of a sudden, disaster will fall upon them as suddenly as a woman's birth pains begin when her child is born. And these people will not be able to get away anywhere—there will be no place to hide.' "*

* The Living Bible

Jim found himself listening intently to this man who had come and prayed for him. It was not only that the pastor had put himself out to help a stranger; the words he spoke seemed to pck up a theme that had begun before the accident. In fact, he had been thinking about this very thing when the snake had struck.

"Now, how can we be sure of this?" the pastor continued. "The dictionary says that prophecy is a declaration of something to come. The Bible contains many prophecies, written long before they came true, which are now history—fact. And it contains many which have yet to be fulfilled. And there is no reason to believe they won't be: the Bible has a pretty good track record.

"Last Sunday we discussed specific prophecies. This morning I want to discuss my understanding of the Scriptures as to the signs of the end times, and the Antichrist. Now it is my belief, based on what I feel the Scripture is saying, that a federation will be formed in the early months after the Lord has returned and taken believers with Him. It may be that the political necessity for self-defense will prompt this move. Some people feel that many nations, such as those which make up Europe, would be unable to defend themselves, and would feel it a necessity to pool their resources, thus beginning the Federated States—or the United States of Europe. Today's news of the Common Market and other alliances is certainly pointing in a direction like this.

"When the time comes for this federation to be

formed, a great leader will come on the scene. A powerful leader. First John says, 'Indeed, many rightly call him the Antichrist.'

"He will be an instrumental in establishing peace in the beginning, but will be a man of evil—against God.

"Some people are of the opinion that if Christ were to return in the next thirty years, this man could very well be alive today."

"I am the Antichrist!" Jerry's words echoed through Jim's mind from the picnic many weeks past. He shuddered slightly and shifted in the pew to hide the uncontrolled reaction. Jenny and Susan both smiled at him, and the attention of all three went back to the pulpit.

"If Jesus were to return even sooner, this man could be active in politics at this very moment.

"I have talked with many Christian friends about the rapture of the church of Christ and have been amazed at the number of stories of people coming home and seeing evidences of loved ones who had just been there and were gone. A friend from my last pastorate back East tells of a hot night when he awoke, took off his pajama top, and went downstairs for a cool drink of iced tea. His wife rolled over and was awakened by the fact that he wasn't next to her. She switched on the light, and all that she saw was his pajama top!"

A light ripple of laughter bounced around the congregation. But there were those, like Susan, whose imaginations were working on the reality of the story. She moved closer to her sister, and Jenny, not knowing what was on her mind, smiled, and put her arm around her.

"Well, again we have seen in our studies the past few weeks," Pastor Belevedere was finishing his sermon, "that there are more prophecies about the end times being fulfilled today than ever before. It is my firm belief that no one has much time left to join the followers of Jesus Christ."

Jim was quiet as he moved with the crowd past Pastor Belvedere at the door. "Nice to see you again. How are you feeling?" the pastor asked. Jim replied with the expected cordiality and hurried away.

Jenny had wanted to introduce him to her parents, but he was gone.

* * *

"Mom! I'm home!" It was later in the afternoon, and Susan had just come in from play. "Sandy had to go to her aunt's, and nobody else—" She stopped.

The house was unusually quiet. Susan was standing in the living room, and suddenly a feeling of being strangely alone crept through her. She leaned as far as she could without falling, trying to see into the kitchen; but she was not in a good place, so she had to walk in.

On the stove, something was burning. The table was partly set, but there was a napkin and a fork and spoon on the floor.

It's happened! her mind screamed at her. *It's happened, and you're left here all alone!* Panic gripped Sue, and she began to scream. Long, pained screams bounced off the walls back at her and only made her scream the harder.

She ran into the living room, screaming. She ran upstairs to the bedrooms, screaming. But all the running and screaming did nothing but convince her she was indeed all alone and would be forever.

She started to run downstairs again and tripped near the top of the stairs. She knew she was falling; and, with one last scream, she shut her eyes and waited to be hurt when she hit.

But the hurt never came. She fell into something soft and warm. The thought flashed through her that she might have just been killed and God took her in after all.

"Easy, sweetheart," a deep, friendly voice said. If it was the voice of God, it sure sounded like her father. She opened her eyes, and she was being held in his strong arms. He had somehow caught her as she fell.

Seconds later, her mother and sister were at the stairs, and everyone was talking at once. "What happened, baby?" her mother questioned.

"What's wrong?" Jenny asked, touching her arm.

Susan looked at them all, groggily, as though just waking up, and was able to say, "I thought you were gone. I thought you were gone," before the uncontrollable sobs came. "I thought—I thought I waited too long," she wept. "I thought you were all gone."

Another hour and a few cups of hot chocolate later, Susan was able to stop shivering. When a tremor hit, she tried to laugh. "How can I be chilly on a hot day like this?"

"You've had a terrible shock, baby," her mother said, soothingly.

"All this talk about the end times and all, just isn't good for young imaginations," her father said, trying to be light.

"But isn't it all true, Daddy?" Susan asked.

"Well—yes, I guess it is. But—"

"I don't want to be left behind."

"Sh, honey," her mother said. "We know you don't. We'll talk about it when you feel better."

"But that might be too late."

"What are you trying to say, Sue?" Jenny asked, sensing that something specific was weighing her sister down.

"I knew for a long time that I should ask Jesus into my heart. But I thought I could just do it anytime. And then, today—"

"It's all right now, honey."

"But it isn't all right, Mom," Susan protested. "It's not all right until I *do*—until I *know* that I won't be left all alone."

"You can do that right now," Jenny said quietly. "Right here. If you want to."

There was a pause in which they all looked at Susan, and then she said, "I want to. I want to ask Jesus into my heart right now." And she did. As simply as a child does such things. She said, "Lord Jesus, please come into my heart. I know You died for me, like the preacher—and like my sister—says You did. And I know that You love me. And I want to really love You. So please save me and come and live in my heart. Amen. Oh, and thank You. Amen."

There were tears of joy on Jenny's face that afternoon, as there were again on an afternoon not too many weeks later, as she laughed and threw handfuls of rice on a dodging, laughing Jim and Patty Wright. The car, announcing "Just Married," was waiting at the curb; but there were many well-wishing bursts of rice to run through before they were safe inside.

Jenny, Dave, and Pastor Belevedere were there, although the wedding took place in Patty's church, and Pastor Belevedere was only a guest. Jerry and Diane were there; Jerry was, at the moment, holding an imaginary microphone, and doing his rendition of Clem McCarthy announcing a horse race. "They're rounding the final turn and heading for home! Patty is in the lead! No, Jim is! No, Patty! Not bad action for a slippery rice track!"

There were laughs and shouts that continued after the doors slammed and the new Wrights were safely away from the rice storm. The engine was started, and just before they drove off, the Reverend Mr. Turner, who had tied the knot, walked to the car and signaled that the window be lowered. He obviously had some parting wisdom, and Patty rolled it down.

"I just wanted to say," he entoned with much practiced sincerity, "the best of luck to both of you."

And they were off! Jim had found a funny card which he had given Patty. It said, "Just think! Two weeks of fun and frolic! And then—" and inside the card it said, "Well, let's try not to think about that."

It was a magnificent two weeks, as she and Jim walked, hiked, swam, lounged, discovered. There was music everywhere, or at least Patty thought so. It was as though, for a short time, all the smog in the world had lifted, and everything looked clearer, shinier, more deeply colored, more dazzling.

It was not until they were driving back home to their new apartment that a tiny frown line appeared between Jim's eyebrows.

"What's the matter?" Patty asked.

"Huh?" Jim responded, with his eyes still on the road. "What do you mean?"

"Don't try to fool me, Jim Wright," Patty said, trying to sound stern but not achieving it. "We've been married long enough for me to know when something's bothering you. You're tired of me. That's it, isn't it?"

Jim turned to kiss her, but the car started to swerve, so he stopped and just laughed at her. They drove a while longer, and finally he said, "There is one thing—"

"I knew it!"

"Where do you think we should go to church?"

The question was so far from left field that it took Patty a full thirty seconds even to believe it. "It doesn't matter to me at all," she said finally. "There. Does that ease your mind?"

"I wasn't really—" Jim started but never finished.

* * *

"Do waffle irons ever wear out?" Patty shouted from the kitchen area of the apartment. There was only an oven, a stove, a refrigerator, and a counter, but it was relatively clear of boxes and suitcases.

"What?" Jim answered, coming from the bedroom. "I didn't hear you. I was trying to put up my tie rack. I didn't know they put metal frames around closets. The way it's painted, you can't even tell, but it sure won't take a screw. What did you say?"

"Thank you for that moment of your consciousness." Patty hugged him. "I just asked if waffle irons ever wear out."

"Beats me. But they do keep making new ones. Why?"

"We have two of them."

"Two waffle irons?"

"From a cousin of mine and from someone whose name I don't even recognize. Probably a friend of yours. And there must have been a sale. They're both the same brand and model."

"Keep one wrapped up. We'll give it to somebody who's getting married."

"Good idea. Let *them* worry about what to do with two!"

"If Jerry were here," Jim added, "He'd probably say something like, 'How waffle!' "

They laughed, and Jim started back toward the bedroom.

"Wait a minute," Patty called, and Jim stopped. "I'm going to keep them both."

"What for?"

"I want to be married to you long enough to *use*

them both. Let's see how long it takes to wear one out."

Jim came back to her, and they embraced. "Oh, my sweet," he said, quietly. "Oh, my sweet. May it be." And then the same little frown line intruded and left again.

"There it is again," Patty said, still in his arms.

"What?"

"It's a little line that pops up between your brows. What were you thinking about just then?"

"Oh." Jim was obviously pushing the moment away. "Nothing, really."

"I mean it. What?" Patty insisted.

"I was just thinking about—well, about time."

"Time," she responded flatly. "Interesting," she said with an attempt at the voice of an analyst. "And how long has this thinking about time troubled you?"

"It's a little more serious than that, Patty."

Patty pulled back a little from him, but stayed in his arms. "What do you mean?"

"I just can't seem to get that stuff about the end of the world— You know?"

"All that religious business that Jenny and her friends talk about?"

"That's right. I just can't seem to get it out of my mind. I mean, if it's really true, I—I just don't know."

Patty was now really concerned with his feelings. "What do you want to do about it?"

"I don't know. Maybe talk to somebody."

"Like who?"

"Like maybe that minister that was at the hospital.

61

I—uh—I went to his church once. He seems like he's all right."

"Well, honey, if you feel like it's the thing to do, why don't we have him over? The place is still a disaster area, and we've got practically no furniture, but I don't think ministers are supposed to mind."

Jim's attitude relaxed, and he doused Patty with a smile. "Thanks."

Patty hugged him. "I'd do anything to see that smile."

Jim gave her one more quick hug and started back toward the bedroom. Then he stopped, and turned back to Patty, who was still watching him with a warm look. "I wonder," he said.

"What?"

"How long it *does* take to wear out a waffle iron."

FIVE

"I don't think I've ever had waffles at this time of the evening," Pastor Ed Belevedere said, as he poured syrup on the steaming waffle in front of him. He, Jim, and Patty were sitting in the living room, each with a waffle on a plate on the coffee table. The pastor was in the only chair, while Patty and Jim sat on the floor.

"You almost didn't have one tonight," Patty responded. "The first one stuck so tight I thought I'd never get it out."

"You should have switched to the other iron," Jim winked.

"I thought of that," Patty smiled. "But then I figured if the first one stuck in one, it'd stick in the other. Anyway, they say you should throw away the first waffle, so I scraped it out, and everything seems to be working all right now."

"I'll say," the pastor said enthusiastically. "Delicious!"

The brief discussion of waffles was designed to lighten the atmosphere a little. Pastor Belevedere and Jim had been deep in a discussion of sin, justice, and the sacrifice of the Son of God. There had been a heavy, thoughtful pause, and the pastor thought waffles might be a good change of pace in the talk. But now it was obvious to all three that the waffle thing was played out, and the discussion had to continue.

"What do you think about all this, honey?" Jim turned to Patty.

"Frankly, it's all beyond me. I don't know how seriously to take any of it. I've been raised in the church, taught to do the best I can, believe in God, and hope everything works out. I'm good. I don't steal or cheat. I'm as good as the next person. Maybe better. What else is there?"

Pastor Belevedere sat back in his chair. He wished, momentarily that he was not sitting on a higher level than his two young friends. His expression helped bridge that distance; it was one of sympathy rather than judgment. He smiled. "You know, if I had a nickel for every time I've heard somebody say that, I'd be a rich man today. But, you see, Patty, God made you for Himself. He made us so that we might enjoy Him and each other together. But we—you broke up that relationship by choosing not to include Jesus Christ."

Patty stiffened slightly. "I never made a choice like that."

"Have you ever chosen *for* Him?"

"Well, no. I guess not. But my minister says we get all hung up with theology. God is love. He's not going to destroy us when we can't even help doing wrong things once in a while, is He?"

"I wish I could agree with you, Patty. Believe me, I do. It'd make my job a whole lot easier. But the Bible is full of examples to the contrary, starting with the first sin and moving right through the history of mankind. Yes, God is love—the greatest love any of us can ever know. But God is also holy, and He does punish sin."

"I think I understand," Jim said from a thoughtful position on the floor. "But where does love fit in? How could a God who loved me, for instance, cause me to go through that whole snake bite thing?"

"There are never simple answers, Jim. But there are principles by which we can look at what happens to us. In this case, I'd start with something like this: God is the Father, something like your own father, let's say. Sometimes He makes you go through things you don't like in order to teach you. When you go through something like you did with Christ, there's good in it. That's a promise straight from God. When you go through it without God, no good needs to come from it.

"I don't quite follow."

"Well, now that I think of it, maybe there *was* something important God wanted you to learn." Pastor Belevedere had been searching for words until now, but he suddenly came alive. "Look at it this way, Jim. How much of a chance did you have when they brought you into the hospital?"

"Not much, they tell me."

"None at all, actually. The fact that you were in good physical condition kept you going longer than

most, but you were a goner. There was no way your body could produce the antibodies needed to to stop that poison.''

Jim began to anticipate what the pastor had realized. He spoke slowly, finding the principle as he said it. "But someone else—that man from Florida—had already gone through it. His blood had the cure.''

"Exactly! *He* had the cure. And all you had to do was *accept* it. You took that man's blood, and it saved your life!''

"I—I never thought of it that way.''

"Jesus Christ died on the cross—shed His blood for you, Jim—Patty—and all you have to do is accept it, just like there in the emergency ward. That man walked in and gave you his blood. Had you turned it down, we wouldn't be having this conversation today. I think—I think the whole human race is in a kind of emergency ward, only we don't know it. And Jesus says, 'My blood can save you from death, if you'll only accept it.' God is offering you eternal, abundant life with Him. You have everything to gain, Jim, and absolutely nothing to lose. All you have to do is ask Him.''

In the long pause that followed, Jim sat, staring at the floor, in deep turmoil. Patty watched him with strange, conflicting feelings. In one way, she wanted him to make this decision to follow Christ. She knew, from conversations they had been having, that it was strongly on his mind. And making the decision would

ease his mind and free him from whatever seemed to be just out of reach, haunting him.

On the other hand, she was not sure she wanted him to go this far with religion. There was something exclusive about people who called themselves Christians. "In the Bible sense of the word," they'd always say. They somehow brought God into everything, and made others feel uncomfortable. If making this decision would do something like that to Jim, she did not want it.

"Man, things sure have been moving fast," Jim finally said. "There's a lot in me that says what you're saying is right."

"I believe God has been speaking to you for a long time, Jim."

"But why would He go through all this just to have me?"

"Why would He die for *any* of us?" the pastor responded. "That's all part of what we discover after He's moved in and begun working with us. It has to do with the love you were asking about."

"I—I guess if He's gone so far, I'd better listen to what He's saying."

Pastor Belevedere smiled. "Yes, I guess you'd better."

There was a momentary pause in the room, like the moment a swimmer is in the air before bouncing off the diving board into the pool. Then Jim jumped. "Okay. I believe it. I'm ready."

That night, after the pastor left, there was very little conversation between Jim and Patty. Patty had watched as Jim prayed, inviting Jesus to move in an take his life. She had seen the expression of great relief come over him, an expression she had seen before only in their closest moments together. She had felt a little jealous, a little skeptical, and a little ashamed at having to say to the pastor, "No. I'm not ready for something like that yet."

"Just leave the dishes. I've got nothing else to do tomorrow," Patty said to Jim, as he started stacking the sticky plates.

They prepared for bed separately, passing once or twice in the hall between the bedroom and bathroom, and exchanging the kind of a smile strangers exchange in the same situation at a boardinghouse or ski lodge.

"Aren't you going to pray, or something?" Patty asked Jim as he sat on the edge of the bed.

"You know," he responded, a slight irritation to his tone, "this is ridiculous! You're treating me like I'm some kind of visitor."

"*I'm* treating *you*?" Patty snapped back, more quickly than she had expected to. "I haven't heard you being exactly cordial and outgoing since your—whatever it was."

Jim sighed, and his voice warmed. "Patty, honey, we're making something out of this that we shouldn't. Look at us. We're actually having something that sounds like the start of an argument."

"God is love," Patty pouted.

"Honey," Jim implored. "Let's not let this happen.

Okay, so I did what I felt was the right thing to do *for me*. I'm not pushing you, am I? I'm not forcing anything on you."

"No," Patty admitted. "But you have some kind of a holy look, or something. I saw the same thing on Jenny's face when she—when she did what you did. It makes me feel like you have something—I don't know—more important, or something."

"More important than what, baby? Try to put it in words."

"Oh, Jim, I'm jealous—of God! I think He took you away from me tonight."

Jim wrapped her in his arms and spoke very quietly. "It doesn't work that way, Patty. I don't know how to say this exactly, but I think I love you *more* because of tonight. I see you—somehow differently. And I want so much for you."

Patty shook her hair and tears out of her eyes and looked at him for a long time. "Oh, Jim, don't let your religion come between us. Please."

"I hope you'll share it with me someday."

"But if I don't—if I can't—if I just can't get psyched up enough to think that it's all really true, you won't leave me, will you?"

"Leave you?" There was a small degree of hurt in Jim's voice.

"You're going to start seeing people—like Jenny—who really is sweet and believes the way you do—and I'm afraid you'll just think I'm—"

"Sh," Jim whispered. "Know what I really think?"

"What?"

70

"I think when you see how neat it is to live with God inside you, you'll come over. I can't tell you how I feel inside, but I hope you'll see. And when you do, we'll have it all together."

"But I might not, Jim," Patty almost wailed. "I might just stay the way I am."

"With God loving you, and me loving you, you don't stand a chance," Jim smiled and touched her nose with his finger.

They lay in silence for a few minutes, and then Patty ventured a hesitant, "Jim?"

"Uh-huh?"

"If you do pray, will you pray for me?"

"Every time I see you or think about you."

"Do I need it that much?" she asked, and her simple sincerity sent Jim into a long, warm laugh.

"Good night, my sweet," he said at length.

"Good night, my love," she answered.

They both stared at the ceiling for a long time before dropping off.

* * *

"Sue, will you run next door and ask Mrs. Thompson if I could borrow a stick of margarine?" Jenny was trying to make muffins for breakfast before her parents came downstairs, but she was short of supplies. Her sister, who was always there to clean bowls with her fingers, started toward the door.

"You be sure to be here when I get back," she said with a smile.

"Don't worry, sweetie. If I'm gone, you will be, too."

71

As Susan crossed the driveway between their home and the neighbors', the strangeness of light quality drew her attention to the sky. It was a different kind of morning. The clouds seemed to be moving faster than she had ever seen them travel. But there was no perceptible breeze on the ground. She looked and thought it was unusual and beautiful, and made a mental note to ask Jenny what caused things like that.

In another part of town, someone else was looking at the strange sky. Dave had been up early in order to mow the lawn. He was to have a rehearsal with his singing group that afternoon, and the lawn was the only requirement in his way.

Now he stared at the clouds. At first they made him think it was going to rain, but the leaves on the trees were all right-side-up, and, like Susan, he was puzzled by the fact that there was no breeze.

"Well," he said to himself with a shrug. "I might as well get as much done as I can before it comes down." And he bent over the mower and pulled the cord, starting the engine.

Pastor Ed Belevedere was bending over at that moment. He was in front of the church, the glass front of his signboard open, and letters strewn about on the ground in front of him. He had put the word "THE" up, and was searching for another E when his attention, too, was called to the strange movements in the sky.

He looked up, shielding his eyes from the brightness. But there seemed to be no effective way to do it.

The brightness seemed to be coming from the whole sky at once. The pastor squinted and then decided that the cloud cover must be dispersing the sun's rays unusually evenly. He went back to his search for the next E. And he continued squinting.

Patty stirred only slightly as Jim rolled out of bed and started down the hall toward the bathroom. It was only habit that made him turn on the bathroom light. He saw immediately that he did not need it. The light coming in through the frosted window was almost too much.

He turned on his electric razor and smiled at himself in the mirror. Of course the day would appear brighter. He had new life—straight from God—and it felt good. He almost thought he heard a kind of musical sound, and again he smiled. He knew it must be his imagination, that if he turned off his razor, the sound would be gone, like the many times he had been shaving and thought he had heard a phone ring.

Again the strong light from outside called for his attention. It was so bright, even through that small translucent window, that he wished he had a curtain to pull. "That's some light, Lord," he said, half joking. "I don't think I've ever really noticed it before."

And then it was gone. The morning light seemed almost dark by contrast. The clouds sat still again, and all returned to what seemed normal.

Only a few things, here and there, were out of place. On the driveway between the neighbors' and Jenny's houses, a stick of margarine melted. At the

73

end of three rows of freshly cut grass, a mower sat, its engine roaring but going nowhere. The signboard in front of Pastor Belevedere's church still had letters scattered around on the ground beneath it, but no one was there to finish the sentence that began "THE END IS."

SIX

"The event spoken of in the Hebrew-Christian Scriptures is described somewhat in the gospel of St. Matthew, chapter twenty-four, verses thirty-six and on," the announcer's words continued out of the clock radio, bringing Patty out of her reverie and back to the present.

It was really happening. All those things that she had heard about and pushed to one side were happening. Right now. And she was still here. Alone.

"Jesus Christ is reported to be the speaker and says, and I quote, 'But of that day and hour knoweth no man, no, not the angels of heaven, but my Father only. But as the days of Noe were—' Uh, this just in from news central, the UN has established a special emergency committee and will be making an unprecedented worldwide radio and television simulcast at noon today. The purpose of this broadcast will be to assess the world situation and establish methods and procedures for handling possible problems and dangers facing the world in this crisis."

Patty reached over and shut off the radio, then

slumped back down beside the bed. She wanted to cry but did not have the energy. There was a kind of heavy, almost drowsy acceptance coming over her. She remembered the feeling; she had had it in school when she had studied all night and knew she was not ready for the exam. There was nothing more to do. It was hopeless.

She must have dozed, because when she again looked at the clock radio, it was just one minute till noon. She stood, feeling the stiffness of staying in one position too long, and she stumbled down into the living room. She had the feeling of being an actor in a very tragic drama. It was as though she had rehearsed every move; and although she did not feel like going through it, she seemed to have to.

The living room was dark. The drapes had not been pulled back to allow the day in. Patty turned on the small television set and sat on the one chair, pulling her legs up close. The pale blue light from the set only accented the cold emptiness of the room.

"Ladies and gentlemen," a tall, graying man with sharply handsome features was speaking from a room at the UN. "As I speak to you this day, my words are being translated into every major tongue and dialect in the world. This morning, the United Nations met in an emergency session and formed the organization you see represented by this symbol."

He gestured overhead, and the television camera tilted up to see the large letters, UNITE, on the wall behind his head.

"The United Nations Imperium of Total Emergency," the man explained, and the camera came back down to him. "The Imperium is designed to exercise total world power only as long as the emergency exists. There is an emergency. As yet we have not established the exact nature of this emergency, but UNITE is anxious that all feelings of panic and fear be held in check."

Patty shuddered. So much of what Dave had said on the picnic, so much of what Jenny had said, and what Jim questioned, raced through her mind. No need to panic? Didn't he know? This was only the beginning.

"The Imperium is made up of leaders from six major world powers and consists of six committees of six members each within those countries. The exact function of the various members of the various committees will be explained fully in subsequent news releases through your local newspapers, radio, and television stations.

"You can be sure that the Imperium, while taking absolute control of world government during this emergency, will truly represent your feelings and needs."

"My needs?" Patty said quietly. "I only have one. I need another chance."

"It is because of this potential threat to our entire planet that this one world government, the Imperium, has had to be formed; and each member of the world council wishes to assure those of his fellow citizens that as soon as the emergency is passed, we will return to self-rule for all nations."

"As easy as that," Patty thought. She had at one time sidestepped the whole story on the basis that it would be impossible to bring all the nations of the world together under one umbrella. "Too simplistic," she had thought. "They'd never go along with it." And yet, within a few hours after the "emergency," one world government was fact.

Patty pushed the control button, and the set went black. Now what? She sat in the chair for a long time, not really thinking. She kept remembering scenes that had taken place, words, phrases, concepts that she had missed or had not taken seriously at the time.

Finally she pulled herself out of the chair and walked to the window. She pushed aside the drape just a little and looked out. The day looked normal enough. There was light traffic on the street, and a few people here and there. Everyone she saw seemed to be hurrying a little more than usual, and there were many quick glances up to the sky. "But it's normal to expect anxiety today," Patty thought. She dropped the edge of the drape back in place.

"Jim?" she turned and started to call, and then was hit again with the knowledge that he was not there. "Oh, God! God!" she cried staring at the ceiling. A cobweb swung lazily in the minimal air currents near the ceiling.

* * *

It took a few days for Patty to begin to function again. She spent those days walking through the apartment's three rooms, sometimes crying, sometimes sitting in a hypnotic stupor, sometimes trying to force time back with her mind. But finally, she knew she had to start some kind of life again. She began with a long bath, and then dressed. It was more of an effort than she had thought it would be. *Come on, Patty,* she urged herself. *You've got to make the best of it.* And she struggled hard to stop the thought that flew into her mind, shouting, *There is no best of it!*

She began to clean the bedroom. She knew she would have to clean the whole apartment, but she did not as yet feel up to tackling the remains in the living room of the visit of Pastor Belevedere. There were too many phrases, too many fresh memories from that evening.

The bedroom done, she went into the bathroom. Jim's razor still lay in the sink where she had pulled it from the wall plug. It seemed so heavy when she lifted it from the sink. She stared at the little collection of black dust in the bottom of the sink—all that was left on earth of Jim, of their marriage, of beauty. Patty held the razor to her cheek for a few moments, and then, seeing herself in the mirror looking so sad, so melodramatic, she threw the razor in the wastebasket. "I feel like God has taken you away from me," she had said to him that night.

"Why didn't You—?" she started to shout at the ceiling again. But she knew the answer before the question was formed. The thought came back as a quiet, steady answer, *Why didn't you?*

With a resolute sigh, she entered the living room,

79

opened the drapes, and began to clean. "I've got nothing else to do," she had told Jim when he started clearing after the visit.

The dishes were stacked in the sink, and the napkins were thrown away. The Bible still lay on the floor where the pastor and Jim had dug for phrase after phrase that night. Patty remembered how good Jim looked when he was that intense. She picked up the Bible. It was open somewhere in the middle, and her eyes caught just a few words as she closed it. "Today if ye will hear his voice, harden not your heart as in the—" She suddenly wanted to read more, to finish the sentence, but it was closed, and she knew she would never find it again. *And why should I?* she said to herself. *Dave said that when all this took place, that was that.*

She laid the Bible on the boards-and-bricks bookshelf that she and Jim had just finished putting together before the pastor's visit. She walked into the kitchen to wash the dishes.

"I want to be married to you long enough to use them both." Her words came to mind as she picked up the waffle iron. And that was it for the morning. Patty cried a long time in the kitchen.

In every hopeless situation there is the feeling that if only one does enough suffering or penance, the situation will change. There was some of that feeling in Patty's weeping. *It can't be too late*, her thoughts would plead. And then they would answer, *It is.*

It was sometime in the afternoon of the third day that Patty finished the apartment and began to realize that she had not eaten in that time. *I can't stay here,* she thought. *Maybe getting out and seeing what the rest of the world is doing will help.*

It was obvious that make-up would not hide her days of crying, but the funny, big sunglasses Jim had bought for her on their honeymoon would. *Why does everything relate to Jim?*

The air smelled good as she stepped from the building. She made a mental note to open a few windows when she returned. The sunlight felt warm on her skin. It was good to hear the sounds of traffic and people doing things.

The little restaurant was only a few blocks away, and in that walk, Patty began to feel more alive—even hungry. Could it all have been a dream, or some gigantic joke? Maybe somehow Jerry and Jim had conspired to put her on, and the disappearance and the radio and television broadcasts were really part of the joke? Maybe Jim and Jerry were watching her, breaking up over the success of their scheme. She looked around quickly but saw no one who looked the least bit familiar.

At the corner, the newsstand still had all the usual newspapers and magazines. She had not noticed how many pornographic magazines the stand carried. Perhaps it was because they were now in a more prominent place. The headlines caught her eye. One paper said, *UNITE Appoints World Leader,* and another, *UNITE Leader Assures: Not A "Big Brother."*

No, it was not a dream or a put-on. It had really

happened. It *was* really happening. And she was still here. The tears began to well up again, but this time Patty stopped them. Crying was all right when you were alone.

She ate at the counter in the restaurant. And as she ate, she became aware of a difference. The restaurant was quiet, except for the occasional clink of silver on china. She looked around, and everyone was eating in silence. There was a mechanicalness about the scene. Even at those few tables where more than one person sat eating, there was silence. A reach for the salt or catsup by one person seemed to evoke an irritated look from another. Nothing was said, and there were no smiles.

* * *

"Well! You're in the land of the living!" Diane's voice on the phone was the first chipper sound Patty had heard. She had finally worked up the nerve to call and see who was still alive. Diane was. "So is Jerry," she continued. "In fact, sweetie," Diane dropped into her familiar sultry tones, "he's living right here."

Patty's reaction surprised even herself. In the past, she might have simply let the comment and the situation go. She did not agree with it, but she did not feel it right to impose her standards on others. Now she was repelled. The realization that what the Christian faith had to say was actually true, had changed her whole point of view. It was no longer a live-and-let-live situation; it was a situation where values, standards, morals were important.

She was about to react with a plea for Diane to break away from the relationship with Jerry, when she realized that now it really *did not* matter. The hope for good, for justice, for right, was gone from the world. As Dave had said at the picnic, "It's a whole new ball game. Only this time with no rules."

"How's Jim? Diane's voice cut through Patty's thoughts.

"Oh, he's—he's fine," Patty said, trying to keep her voice from cracking.

"We'll have to get together, Patty. Real soon. Just because everybody else in the world is scared to go outside, that doesn't mean we have to sing funeral dirges, does it?"

"Yeah. Sure, Diane. Let's do it. Soon." Patty's voice trailed off as she replaced the receiver. She sat for a long time, looking out of the window. It was a strange feeling for her. She was left behind, but she was not like the others. Not like Diane and Jerry and all those who were still here who did not know or believe what had really happened. She now knew that it was true—the whole Christian thing. But there was nothing she could do about it. Where in the past, she had enjoyed Diane's loose approach to life, now she felt sickened by it. And she knew that only people like Diane were left.

She had discovered too late that the loving God, who had allowed the world to go on as long as He had just so that as many as would could come to Him, had finally called a halt and moved into the next phase. She had discovered that the straight way was the only way. And now she was straight in a crooked world.

As the days passed, Patty's thoughts reached in all directions, trying to decide what to do. *Why not give in to it? There's no reason not to let down now. Live a little. There's no more threat of punishment; the punishment has begun. You might as well do something really wild now, since you'll end up in hell anyway.*

But her mind was too disciplined for that. She had always been good, and there was no way she could justify reprobate behavior now. There was still something called personal worth.

Well, if you don't fit in the world as it is now, why wait around? It's a simple matter to slash your wrists. Do it under running cold water; you'll never feel it. You know you're only in conflict with the way things are. You're entire existence will be torture from now on. Why not get to the end as quickly as possible? Do it!

And she almost did. But the razor blades were in the medicine chest next to Jim's after shave, and the smell of him stopped her.

Her mind scratched desperately for hope. *Maybe—maybe the fact that I am not falling in with the way things are—maybe that means there's still a possibility for me. Maybe if I try to live—* It was slim, but it was something to hang onto.

And as the weeks passed, she found herself needing more and more to hang onto. The incidence of crime steadily rose, according to the papers. In a time of unprecedented world peace, local crimes were up. It became unwise to go out after dark; bands of restless men seemed to be roaming like packs of dogs around the streets.

UNITE finally brought all local police authority under its control, in an effort to stop the rising crime rate. And night after night, Patty watched from the window of her darkened apartment as UNITE vans with loudspeaker systems reminded the population to tune in to the messages.

"It is just a simple necessity that each of us *identify* with UNITE and fully support its progress and strategy. Before the emergency, we were at each others' throats. Let us continue to make world-wide unity the positive result of our common dilemma. Report today to your local UNITE Identification Center, and show yourself a true citizen of the world."

This was the latest in a series of plans to come from the Imperium. For the past month, much had been said about the achievement of world peace, contrasted by tremendous breakdown of law and order at the local level. The Imperium had suggested that the negative elements in society might well be the agents of the outside enemy, or whatever had caused the emergency in the first place. "We must not let these elements destroy us from within," the Imperium had announced. "We must discover the source of the irritation and remove it."

In line with this, UNITE had come up with a simple plan. A patriotic gesture which would show a man to

be behind UNITE all the way. It was a tattoo, a mark, and it was to be inscribed into the skin in a place where it would always be visible. The mark was small, and not gaudy in its appearance. It was a box, and inside were three sets of numbers directly over each other:

```
0110
0110
0110
```

The length of the line in front of the UNITE Identification Center surprised Patty. She stood across the street from what was once Pastor Belevedere's church and watched as person after person went in, and came out with the mark.

The emergency had left a number of churches with so few in the congregation that they had closed. The few members who remained attended one of the churches which had not been affected. The vacant churches, like Belevedere's, were ideal places for setting up UNITE centers.

"Back of the hand, or forehead?" the bored UNITE worker asked a pretty young girl who was there with her boyfriend.

"Will it wash off?" the girl asked coyly.

The UNITE worker had been at her desk all day and was lacking in patience. "It's permanent," she snapped, sobering the girl.

"Oh, you'd better put it on the back of my hand," she said quietly.

At the next table, a squarely built man with graying hair was gesturing proudly to his forehead.

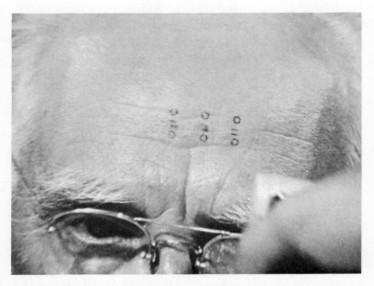

"Put it right there! I'm not ashamed to be a good citizen!"

Patty had waited in line with the others, wanting to see what was happening inside. Now, just seven places away from the desks, she dropped out of line and pushed her way through the entrance. A quick look was exchanged between a UNITE worker behind his desk and one of the many men who seemed to be standing idly behind the desk area. Without a word, the man slipped out a side door of the church and watched as Patty hurried away toward her apartment.

SEVEN

"It can only be assumed by the Imperium that those in civilized centers of the world who have refused to be identified are working against the goals and purposes of the Imperium."

Patty sat in a position which was familiar to her now, hunched in the living room chair, legs pulled up close to her, watching the latest simulcast from the Imperium.

In the weeks that had passed, the Imperium had made surprising progress in uniting the world. The tattoo seemed to be on everyone, and the common name with which people greeted each other was "citizen."

"Indeed," the Imperium's authoritative speaker continued, "perhaps even in cooperation with the forces which brought about the emergency. It has, therefore, been declared by our leader that, in the interests of world security, all people who do not bear the mark of UNITE will be subject to arrest and prolonged inconvenience."

Patty sighed a long, weary sigh. "I should have known," she half whispered. "It's happening. Just like they said."

"In order that the Imperium may quickly apprehend those who are not in sympathy with its direction, aś of tomorrow morning, all stores, shops, and places of business will be prohibited to sell or give service to any customer unless that customer bears the mark of UNITE. Shopkeepers, clerks, and all employees are required to make known the identity of anyone attempting to transact business without the mark. The Imperium wishes all citizens to understand that this is purely a safety measure, and—" his sincere tones were cut off as Patty pushed the off button.

"Oh, God," she cried out in the darkened room. "Oh, God, why didn't I? Why did I just—"

Her sentence was cut short. A sharp knock at the door, first startled, then froze her with fear. She stood where she was, hands still up in the air, midgesture.

Another sharp rap at the door, and a few exchanged muffled words in the hallway outside the door. She could not make out what was said, but there were at least two men, maybe three.

After what seemed hours, she heard the sound of footsteps fading away from her door. Patty lowered her arms, took what felt like the first breath in all that time, and made her way to the window which overlooked the street.

Below, two men in military dress walked from the apartment building and climbed into a waiting jeep. The markings on the jeep were of UNITE. They exchanged a few more words, then both looked up at

90

Patty's window. She pulled her face back, away from the window. Then slowly she edged forward again to see what they were doing.

They were still looking up. After what seemed another hour, they looked away, picked up what appeared to be a clipboard with a many-page list attached, made a notation by one of the names—hers, Patty was sure—and drove away.

For the first time since the actual morning of the disappearance, Patty felt panic rising within her. There was no way to accept the idea that she was going to be hunted like a criminal! "That day of the Lord will come unexpectedly like a thief in the night. When people are saying, 'All is well, everything is quiet and peaceful'—then, all of a sudden, disaster will fall upon them as suddenly as a woman's birth pains begin when her child is born. And these people will not be able to get away anywhere—there will be no place to hide."

No place to hide! The words echoed from the past through her mind. *No place to hide!* She could not stay in the apartment. Soon the food would run out. And she could not buy food without the mark. The mark of UNITE. The mark of the *beast*, Dave had called it.

Her mind searched for some possibility—some way she might live without the mark—without giving in. But every alley was blind. There was an informer pointing at her bare wrists. There was a UNITE militia man holding open the back door of a paddy wagon. No place to hide!

91

It was after midnight when Patty decided to go out. She had paced back and forth in her dark apartment since early evening when the soldiers had been there. She had been to the window seemingly hundreds of times, startled by every flash of car lights, every siren, every sound of footsteps. Now quiet had settled on the city, and she had to breathe fresh air.

The air was chilly as well as fresh, but it felt good to be moving in an area larger than nine-by-twelve. Patty walked without being conscious of where her walk was taking her. In her mind she groaned, she searched, she went back over plan after plan. But there was always an informer or a paddy wagon. *Huh,* she thought ruefully, *They should call it the Patty wagon.*

Then, suddenly, she was atingle with fear. She had just turned a corner, and not ten feet away were the two militia men in their jeep. In a split second, she was into the bushes which lined the sidewalk. They had not seen her.

As she watched, the two climbed out of their jeep, compared the address with one on their clipboard list, and walked toward the house. The banging on the front door sounded exactly like it had on her door.

Inside, someone turned on a light. *Stupid!* Patty thought.

"Yes? What is it?" the elderly woman who opened the door asked. She was obviously trying to wake up, and she clutched her robe tightly around her.

"Mrs. Livingstone?" one of the militia men snapped, his words sounding very much like the banging on the door.

"Yes," the woman answered, dubiously.

"UNITE," the soldier said. "You're to come along with us."

"At this hour," the woman asked gently. "Oh, I hardly think—"

"Come along," the soldier emphasized, and took the woman by the arm.

"Young man, that hurts," the elderly woman said quietly.

But there was no reprieve. They led her, protesting, down the sidewalk and into the jeep. And just before they pulled away, Patty saw them hand-cuff the woman to a rail in the back seat.

After the sound of the jeep had faded away, Patty

stepped from the bushes. The sidewalk was lit by the light coming from inside the house through the open front door. Patty's first impulse was to go in, shut off the light, close the door, try to find out who the old lady was, and help in some way. But she stopped herself. Someone had told them about the woman. Perhaps that same someone was watching right now. Perhaps a neighbor. Perhaps a relative.

Why would they take a gentle old lady away? What harm could she possibly be? It was crazy. Things seemed to be making less and less sense. "A new ball game," Dave had said. "Only this time with no rules."

Three or four blocks away, a set of headlights turned into the street and began coming her way.

Realizing that she was still standing in the light of the open front door, Patty hurried back into the bushes.

In just a few seconds, another jeep was screeching to a stop in front of the house, and two more UNITE men jumped out. At the same moment, a door opened on a house nearby, and a man came running out. "She ran into the bushes! Right over there!" He shouted and pointed straight at Patty!

She saw the soldiers turn and start running toward her; and after that, there was just a rocky, stumbling blur as she ran through unfamiliar yards, bushes, driveways, darting in and out of dark places. Stopping. Listening. Hearing the running footsteps getting nearer. Hearing the men shouting to each other. Trying to hold her exploding breath which burned in her throat from running and from fear.

Finally, her pursuers gave up. She waited silently in the shadow of a garage and watched as the jeep cruised the neighborhood, occasionally reaching out with the finger of its searchlight into some corner where she might be. And then, finally, it was gone, too. Somewhere in the distance, a chime announced that it was four o'clock. The sun would rise soon.

Patty had stood long enough that she was no longer out of breath. She began to sense pain. She had scratched her face, arms, and legs in the chase. The important thing now was to get back home.

Cautiously she left the darkness of her corner and began walking, looking for a street sign to see where she was. She could not remember how far she had walked, or even in what direction. She had no idea

where her running had taken her. She only knew that she had to get back to the safety of her apartment.

But—her thoughts stopped her. *What if they are waiting for me back there? What if they are watching to see when I get there? What if they have someone like that old lady's neighbor keeping an eye out for me?*

She stood for a long time. There really was no place to go—no place to hide. Then the weariness began to set in again. Panic could do nothing about the inevitable. And it did not matter whether one accepted it or not. What had been foretold was going to happen.

Patty walked openly now, not caring whether she was seen. A car passed, but he did not look up. She mused on how cyclic her feelings were. But she felt that this time she had exhausted all hope—that she did not care anymore. That she was willing to simply take what happened with tired acceptance, and pray—no, hope—that it would all be over soon.

The sidewalk widened, and she looked up to see where she was. It was a church. It was *her* church. The church she had spent so many drowsy Sunday mornings in, trying to focus her attention on anything to stay awake.

She stopped and looked at the dark gray stones and the dark stained glass windows. A flutter of bitterness ran through her mind. But it was only a flutter. It was no good blaming anyone else for her being here. She had plenty of opportunity outside those walls. She was about to move on when she saw what she thought was a flicker of light coming from under the heavy oak front door. She looked again, and it was gone. "I'm starting to see things," she told herself and started to go. But there it was again. "Someone *is* in there," she whispered and moved slowly to the door.

It was unlocked and did not creak as Patty pushed it open. It was still dark outside, but it was even darker inside. And there was a sound, at first hard to distinguish, but a little like the laughing you might expect to hear in a haunted house. It was at an extremely quiet level, but it seemed to echo through the entire sanctuary.

Patty felt no fear. Perhaps there was none left in her. She closed the door behind her and waited, curious to see what would happen.

Then, somewhere the front, there was a bump. A second later, a flashlight came on, and Patty could see the figure of a man. He had just walked into the end of a pew. He looked as though he had been stumbling around in the dark, but it was hard to see much of him.

The laughing sound was coming from him, but it did not seem so much like laughing, now that Patty could see a little of him. There was something familiar about his size and what little she could hear of his voice.

Suddenly, he dropped to his knees. "Oh, Lord," he wailed, and now Patty knew that the sound she had heard was weeping. "Oh, Lord, are You really gone? Is Your Holy Spirit really taken away? Are we really alone?"

Patty walked toward the kneeling, weeping man, almost afraid to believe what her eyes and ears were suggesting to her. "Reverend Turner?"

On hearing his name called, he jerked around, and Patty saw his face for the first time. She wanted to close her eyes.

The Reverend Mr. Turner, who had always had the right tie and the right word in any given situation, looked to be fifty years older than the last time Patty had seen him. There was a light growth of scrubby beard, and his hair pushed in various directions. Patty had seen pictures of men on skid row, and the man she was looking at now could have easily been one of those men.

But it was the look in his eyes. The Reverend Mr.

Turner had always been a dramatic man, and now, lost and afraid, he looked almost too melodramatic.

"Patty?" he asked, as she came close enough for him to see.

"Yes, Reverend Turner."

Then a look of fear came to his face. "Are you one of them?"

"Them?"

"UNITE."

"Oh," Patty said and sat down. "No."

"But—you are still here?"

"Yes."

Tears came to his eyes. "Oh, God, another one."

"Another?"

"How many? How many have I misled? How many are still here because of me?" He smeared the tears away with the back of his hand and then reached for a Bible lying on the floor. He had apparently dropped it in the bump a few minutes earlier. "It was all here. I read it. I even studied it. I preached about it. I preached that it really didn't matter. How many? How many are still here because of me?"

Patty knew that in one sense he was right. She felt overwhelmingly sorry for this man but could not find words.

"I can't sleep. I can't eat. All I see are those faces that sat out there every Sunday. How many? How many? Because of me."

"You—you don't have the mark?" Patty probed, hesitantly.

"I had it on my heart before it ever happened."

"That isn't good enough!" a new voice snapped through the darkness from behind them. And in a moment they were facing two UNITE militia men. "Let's go."

Turner looked at them and then at Patty, a look of disbelief on his face. "You?"

"I didn't bring them," Patty protested.

EIGHT

"Now dear heart, what's your problem?"

Patty opened her eyes. She had been wakened by the sound of someone sliding back the cell door, but she did not open her eyes, hoping it was all a dream. *Maybe,* she thought, *if I just stay asleep a little longer, it will go away.*

But her opened eyes told her this had been no dream. She really had been taken with the Reverend Mr. Turner to the city jail and had been put into a cell. What she remembered of the night—the soldiers, the chase, the old lady, the weeping minister—all seemed a kind of fuzzy dream. But she *was* in a cell, and there was a police matron standing over her. It had been no dream.

"I—I don't understand," Patty found herself more groggy than she had expected. She sat up as she spoke, bringing her legs over the edge of her cot.

"They tell me you don't want to be identified. I suspect there's just some sort of misunderstanding." She was a large woman who looked like she had had many years' service and knew how to handle any situation. But there was a gentleness to her voice. She was speaking to Patty more mother-to-daughter than cop-to-criminal.

"I know what's going on," Patty said, gathering strength. "It's evil. It may be too late for me, but I'm not joining it."

The woman stood, looking at Patty intently for a moment, and then broke into a warm smile. The matron sat down next to her. "There now, you see? There is a misunderstanding. I knew you weren't a bad girl the moment I laid eyes on you. You're one of those religious freaks, aren't you? You think that the emergency was something called the rapture and that UNITE is the worldwide power of evil—the Beast, and all that sort of thing."

"Patty was stunned to hear this woman lay out, in

a few brief sentences, the terror that had been accompanying her through the dark streets. "You—you know about that?" she stammered.

The warm smile of the woman didn't fade. "Of course. When the emergency happened, every *possible* explanation was explored by computer. And, frankly *that* explanation did go high on the list. But we've since ruled it out." Then holding her hand toward Patty so that her UNITE tattoo was before Patty's eyes, she asked, "Does that look like a 666 to you?"

Patty's mind whirled in confusion.

This was only the second conversation she had had about the disappearance. The first had been last night with the Reverend Mr. Turner. She had said to

herself many times, "It's happened—just the way they said it would." Now, face-to-face with UNITE, somehow she felt like the religious freak she had just been called. Maybe there really was an outside alien emergency. Maybe Jim and the others were still alive, being held captive somewhere. But if so, why were only the Christians taken?

"Your Reverend Turner doesn't believe all that anymore. He's come to see that this terrible evil just doesn't exist."

"Reverend Turner?"

"Certainly. We talked with him earlier this morning, and he's come to see that joining us is really to everyone's best and good interest."

"Reverend Turner," Patty said flatly. It was hard to believe. Her mind projected pictures of the man, crying out in the darkness of his sanctuary. Could UNITE actually have convinced him? Patty wished she had had more sleep. The dullness of her mind made it difficult to think.

"You just come along with me," the matron said, rising, her hand on Patty's arm. It did not hurt Patty, but there was a strength to it that made things go the way the matron wanted them to.

Patty went where she was led, as though sleep-walking. If the Reverend Mr. Turner had joined them, after all he had been through, then what was the sense of resisting further? It was just a tattoo. That was all. Just a little mark, and then all the fear and running would be over.

They walked out into the bright morning sunshine. Patty stopped and squinted.

"Come on," her companion said lightly. "It won't hurt a bit."

Patty shaded the sun from her eyes and looked around. They were walking through a small court-yard with official-looking buildings on all sides. She could see a parking lot between two of them, and a few people walking here and there, all looking pur-poseful and ordinary. But in every case the mark on their hands jumped at Patty. She saw hand after hand with the tattoo indelibly inscribed. For a brief moment, the people seemed to have no faces. She saw only hands.

Patty rubbed her eyes to change the vision; and

when she opened them again, she was watching a workman pushing a canvas-covered wheelbarrow in the direction of one of the buildings. First she saw only the mark on his hand, but suddenly, the light breeze, which she had not noticed before, lifted the edge of the canvas.

She jolted to an abrupt stop, her face frozen in terror!

"Here, what's the matter?" her companion asked and then looked to see what Patty was staring at.

In the wheelbarrow was a body, its head and face badly beaten, the blood still running from many of its wounds. And before the workman had time to stop the wheelbarrow and adjust the canvas, Patty recognized the body. It was the Reverend Mr. Turner!

With a sudden burst of strength, Patty kicked the woman as hard as she could and ran for the parking lot.

The woman fell in an attempt to grab both Patty and her painful shin at the same time. Now, on the ground, she shouted for help; and UNITE militia came immediately from the nearby buildings.

In the parking lot, Patty raced to each of the few cars there, hoping to see a key. There was none. She heard shouts of a few of the soldiers who had begun to chase her.

A long hedge was only a few feet away, and Patty leaped into it. For a moment it resisted her, but suddenly it gave way, and Patty found herself tumbling down a steep cement embankment and landing on a solid cement floor. It hurt. She was stunned. But she got to her feet, and in a moment she was running into what appeared to be a large cememt cave.

"Stop!" a voice somewhere above and behind her shouted. She heard a shot, and something chipped the cement just at the opening of the cave. But in another moment she was inside and protected by the dark.

"She ran into the mouth of one of the storm tunnels," a UNITE soldier was saying into his walkie-talkie. "She gets back in there, we'll never find her."

"Have someone watch that entrance for a while. We'll watch others, too. She *has* to come out sometime," the voice at the other end assured his man.

Inside the tunnel, Patty was moving slowly away from the opening. It was dark, and a trickle of water ran down the middle of the tunnel. She kicked into occasional bits of trash, and slipped now and then on something slimy. But she kept her hand along one wall and let it lead her deeper under the city.

Finally she stopped and listened. There were no sounds of followers. Something was dripping nearby, but with the dark and the echo. it was impossible to know where.

She reached down and felt the dry cement beneath her, and sat to catch her breath and her thoughts. They had "convinced" the Reverend Mr. Turner, all right. They killed him. He had actually held out until death.

From somewhere in the past, a few of his words

107

filtered into her mind. "When one brings to a discussion of this kind, plain old—and I might add God-given—common sense, one sees immediately that those differences which men of old seemed to deem worthy of death, are really dead horses!"

The Reverend Mr. Turner had never deemed anything worth giving his life for. Until now. *Surely,* Patty thought, *Surely there is some provision for someone like that. For someone like me?*

A picture of his bloody face flashed into her mind; she pushed it out. She saw the mark on the hand of the man pushing the canvas-covered wheelbarrow. And as her thoughts grew more gruesome, she remembered an old film about monsters who lived in the sewers of the city. It was not the monsters that came to her mind, but the rats that were forever running around in that film.

Patty jumped to her feet. "I've got to get out of here!" she said aloud, and listened, frightened, as her words echoed in all directions for a long period of time. Her voice scared her, and yet she felt compelled to talk to herself. "They'll be watching the entrance," she whispered and felt a little better when it did not echo as long or as far.

"I'll just follow this tunnel. It has to lead somewhere."

For the next few hours, Patty made her way, one step at a time, groping along the wall, following its every turn. She knew the route was mazelike, but in the dark she had no basis for a sense of direction. Phantoms kept appearing to her. She saw Jim, laughing as he lifted her up and carried her through the front door of their apartment. "Put me down," she had mock-protested. "They only do that in 1930 movies."

"I'll make a star out of you," Jim had laughed; and she felt that, if there were such things as stars in your eyes, he had made them appear in hers.

"Oh, Jim, I'm jealous! I'm just plain jealous—of God! I think He took you away from me tonight." Her words and his expression of warmth and love filled the tunnel as she scratched along.

"It doesn't work that way, Patty. I don't know how to say this exactly, but I think I love you *more* because of tonight."

She saw Jenny, her quiet friend, transformed by her newfound faith and always looking as though the strongest light were coming from behind her—or within her.

Light! That was no specter! That was *real* light, coming from somewhere ahead. Patty could see that the tunnel made a long curve and that at the end of the curve was daylight.

She could see well enough that she did not need to touch the side. She started to run. But she stopped immediately when she heard the noise her running made.

She stood still. What if they were up ahead, watching the entrance? *Well, what if they are?* she answered herself. She could not spend the rest of her life crawling around in the slimy dark down here. *I'll have to take my chances out there,* she told herself and started moving cautiously toward the light.

Fortunately, the afternoon sun did not shine directly into the tunnel, so she was still half-hidden even at the mouth of the tunnel. But her eyes, so long in the total blackness, were protesting terribly.

She did not immediately recognize where she was. But as she became accustomed to the low-angle view, some of the buildings began to look familiar. She was at the north end of town, she thought; and, if her calculations were correct, the road running directly overhead was the one that led out to the dam.

She was on the dark side of the large cement canal; and, if she remembered correctly, there was no sidewalk directly above her. "Chances are, no one would be up there who could get me before I have a chance to run," she said. And if she was chased, she could always climb back down and retreat into the tunnel. She would be safe—at least until the first heavy rain!

It was harder getting up the side than it had been getting down. She slipped and skinned her wrist, but she was past reacting to every little scrape and bump.

With one final effort, Patty pulled herself up to street level. She was across the street from a large supermarket. There was little traffic, and she ran across the street and into the lot.

Almost immediately she saw a jeep with UNITE militia men drive into the lot. They were not looking in her direction, but they were looking through the lot methodically.

Are they looking for me? she wondered. Her mind flashed a picture of the gentle old lady and then one of the Reverend Mr. Turner, and then she dropped between two cars as the men from UNITE looked in her direction.

She heard the jeep stop and the men get out. She peered over the window level of the cars between the men and herself, and she saw them starting in her direction. Crouching, Patty ran down one row of parked cars and across to the other side of the lot.

She looked up again. The militia men were still looking through the area where she had just been. She had arrived at a place very near their parked jeep. "We'll have to get together, Patty. Real soon." Diane's words came from the past. Diane! Maybe she would help. Maybe there was still one place left to hide—and think.

Patty looked around and saw a phone booth near the store. She crept to it, found the change, and dialed her old friend's number, watching the two soldiers on the other side of the lot as they checked the contents of each car. If they were after her, they were convinced that she was hiding in one of the cars.

"Hello?" Diane's voice broke into her jumble of thoughts.

"Oh, Diane, thank— I mean, I'm glad you're there."

"Patty?"

"Yes. Diane, listen, you've got to help me!"

"Where are you?"

"In a phone booth. I need somewhere to go. You've got to—"

"Sure, kid," Diane's voice was quiet and controlled. "We can help you. Can't we help Patty, Jerry?" She called away from the phone. Patty could not make out Jerry's reply, but Diane came back. Patty could almost hear her smile. "Jerry says you're hot—I mean as in *criminal.*"

"I'll explain it all to you when I see you."

"He says we'd better not pick you up in town. We might get in trouble. He says we'll meet you at the dam."

"The dam? How can I get there?"

Diane eased into her droll voice, "Well, Patty, I'd be glad to drive you, but—"

Suddenly Patty saw one of the militia men look in her direction and call to his friend. They were a parking lot away, but they started running.

"Okay! The dam! I'll see you there!" Patty yelled, dropping the phone as she ran out of the booth.

She stood momentarily, looking one way and then the other. She could not get back to the tunnel; the men were between it and her. She was tired. Too tired to outrun them. And she really did not know this neighborhood. She would be caught no matter which way she ran.

Then a sound broke in on her. It was a car motor idling. It was the UNITE jeep! It was her only hope. She ran to the jeep, jumped in, and threw it in gear.

Patty and the jeep leaped out of the lot and into traffic. The soldiers drew their guns, but there were too many moving cars for a clean shot.

The jeep roared through traffic. Motorists who saw it coming pulled to the side, assuming it was on urgent UNITE business. And the same motorists sat, scratching their heads when they saw Patty at the wheel!

Out into the country she drove. The dam was only five miles away, and there she could switch into Jerry's car and come back into the city. They would never expect her to come back. She could hide. She would be safe. For a while.

The afternoon sun was low in the sky as she drove, and suddenly what seemed to be a large cloud cut it off from her entirely. Patty glanced and then jumped

with fear. The "cloud" was a UNITE helicopter, and it was obviously there to stop her!

In a wild move, Patty turned the wheel and sent the jeep careening off the road, down a small enbankment, and into a wooded area. It might have been an effective move, but Patty was not secure in the seat; and as the jeep hit the level ground below the road, she was bounced out, hitting the dirt hard.

The fall knocked the wind out of her, but she knew she would have to run for cover. The helicopter, momentarily confused by the move, was now making a wide turn and would be on her in a matter of seconds.

She pushed herself to a standing position and struggled, nearly strangling from lack of breath, toward a denser clump of trees. The helicopter had now seen her and was flying in a direct line toward where she was trying to run.

With one herculean thrust, she fell into the bushes and rolled in among the trees. The helicopter had to rise sharply to avoid smashing into the trees. Apparently the pilot had been too intent on Patty to see the danger into which he was about to fly.

Patty lay as still as she could, gasping for air. Something on her head was bleeding, and the sticky, wet blood had to be blinked away.

No place to hide! The phrase ran through her mind again, as she wiped her forehead with her sleeve and looked to see it wet with her blood.

The helicopter had made another wide turn and was coming in toward the clump of trees where Patty lay. It was moving carefully, but directly, like a bird of prey zeroing in for the kill.

Patty could see it through the leaves, and she knew that it would only be a matter of time before she would be dead. It was now so close she could see the faces of the men inside, set, angry at having been so close to their own destruction a moment ago. One of them carried what looked like a rifle with a telescopic sight.

Patty tried not to move, but her body was twitching with pain and lack of air. The helicopter turned broadside so that the man with the gun was directly opposite her. It was obvious that he could see her and was getting into position to finish her off. Patty saw this, too, and she wanted to run, to move, to do something; but there was no energy left. She could only lay there and watch as the man raised the rifle and pointed it directly at her.

Patty closed her eyes, and a sense of relief began to move over and through her. It was finally over. Nothing could be as bad as what she had been through. She had lost, but she had gone down fighting.

And then the helicopter was going, lifting up and moving out. No shot. No kill. It simply raised up into the air and left her. In a few moments, there was no sound but the breeze in the treetops.

Patty lay staring at the sky, wondering what had happened. Why the long chase? Why the catch, and then nothing?

After a few minutes she stood and walked out into

the open. There was no sound of pursuers. She looked at herself, half expecting to find a bullet hole,
thinking she might actually be dead and this was
what it was like. She had cuts and bruises, but she
had not been shot. And her tired, bruised body began
to complain about its abuse. No, she was alive.

But why was she alive? What providence was left
in the world that would, for some unexplainable
reason, take her killer away at the moment of kill?
She stood and listened. No footsteps. No jeeps or
planes. Just the breeze, and the quiet, distant roar of
water through the generators at the dam.

The dam! She was almost there! Jerry and Diane
would be waiting. There would soon be a place to
rest. Her body received the news gratefully and
began moving toward the roar. She walked slowly
and painfully. The sun sat on the edge of the earth,
setting afire everything it touched. Patty's long
shadow stretched out beside her. She watched it as
she walked, playing with the idea of whether she
even knew that tired, sad-looking girl.

She climbed the incline to the road. *Why am I
always climbing back to the road?* she thought.
Why does everybody keep bringing me to this bench?
came her words from a hospital scene that
seemed to have happened in a previous life.

The dam was now only a few hundred yards
ahead, and Patty saw Jerry and Diane on the other
side, standing by their car. The sight of them was
renewing, and Patty began running. The road was a
straight line over the dam and to her friends and

their car. She ran, and tears of relief began running down her cheeks. She could see that Diane and Jerry were smiling, too. Diane was laughing.

She was halfway across the dam when everything changed at once. Suddenly, from nowhere, the helicopter was over her head. Behind her, a jeep pulled out from a hiding place in the brush along the edge of the road. And ahead, Patty saw Jerry lift a small walkie-talkie and say something into it. And on the back of his hand was that horrible tattoo.

She stopped, crying in disbelief. "Oh, no! Oh, no, please!"

No place to hide. This was it. Behind her, the jeep was moving slowly toward her down the middle of the road. Above her, the helicopter came so low that the sound was deafening, and the wind it created nearly blew her over. And ahead, Jerry was beckoning as Diane continued to laugh aloud. It was a nightmare!

Patty looked around. Just over the rail, about eight feet down, there was a platform on the side of the dam. She was over the rail in a moment, landing easily on the platform. The water rushed out beside her, its sound drowning that of the helicopter.

She looked up. The rail above was now lined with militia men, Jerry, and Diane. They were all coaxing her to come up. All but Diane. Diane was still laughing.

No place to hide. Patty looked down. Was it one hundred feet? Two hundred? She did not know. But it was a long drop, and the cement dam angled out

below her. There was no way to be sure she would hit the water. And even if she did, it was not more than ten feet deep at the base.

No place to hide. She looked back up, just as Jerry dropped to the platform beside her. He flashed his crooked Humphrey Pushcart smile and mocked, "Stick with me, baby, and we'll get you off easy."

Patty backed away. She had never thought of Jerry as actually evil. But the smile, the voice, the trap that he had set. She could not stand to be on the same—

Then she bumped the rail. It was lower on this platform and hit her legs. She was backing away, and the bump was enough to cause her to lose her balance. She was falling backwards. There was nothing to grab. Nothing to stop her. Nothing—

118

Jerry and those above him were suddenly speeding away from her! Her feet were above her. Then they eased over, and she saw the cement wall and water coming at her too fast to stop. Too fast to—

* * *

Patty lurched up in bed with a jolt! Her face was drained, her hair matted with perspiration.

She looked around the bedroom, trying to brush away the last fingers of sleep.

"The event seems to have taken place at the same time all over the world—just about twenty-five minutes ago," a voice came from the clock radio beside the bed. "Suddenly, and without warning, literally thousands, perhaps millions, of people just disappeared."

Patty was awake now, and her mind raced. A quick look toward the open bedroom door brought the sound of an electric razor to her ears.

"Jim?" Patty called, almost hesitantly. Then, as though summoned by the sound of the razor, she crawled across the bed in a straight line to the open door.

"Jim?" she called louder, almost afraid of the answer she would hear. Still the razor and the announcer droned on.

"Speculation is running high that some alien force from outside our system has declared war on our planet. Some feel it to be a spectacular judgment of God."

Patty made her way cautiously down the hall toward the bathroom. "Jim?" she called again. It

119

was the frightened, quiet call of one who already seemed to know there would be no answer.

Now she was at the bathroom door. She stopped before looking in. It was as though she had gone through the moment before, and this time did not want to find what she was about to find.

And now she looked in. And her face showed that it was as she had expected. In only a moment, her expression grew from total dispair to near hysteria. "Oh, no! No! Please, no! Please! *No-o-o-o!*"